[SH]AKE[SPEARE'S]

ROMEO

&

JULIET

RETOLD BY
MARTIN POWELL

ILLUSTRATED BY
EVA CABRERA

COLORED BY
JORGE GONZAL[EZ]

D1114427

STONE ARCH BOOKS
a capstone imprint

Retold by Martin Powell
Illustrated by Eva Cabrera
Colored by Jorge Gonzalez

Series Editor: Sean Tulien
Editorial Director: Michael Dahl
Series Designer: Brann Garvey
Art Director: Bob Lentz
Creative Director: Heather Kindseth

Shakespeare Graphics is published by
Stone Arch Books, 1710 Roe Crest Drive,
North Mankato, Minnesota 56003

WWW.CAPSTONEPUB.COM

Cataloging-in-Publication Data is available
at the Library of Congress website.

ISBN: 978-1-4342-2563-4 (library binding)
ISBN: 978-1-4342-3448-3 (paperback)

PRINTED IN THE UNITED STATES OF AMERICA IN
STEVENS POINT, WISCONSIN.
112011
006465R

TABLE OF CONTENTS

CAST OF CHARACTERS: .... PAGE 08

ACT 1: .... PAGE 10

ACT 2: .... PAGE 32

ACT 3: .... PAGE 50

ACT 4: .... PAGE 64

ACT 5: .... PAGE 70

SHAKESPEARE

WILLIAM SHAKESPEARE WAS ONE OF
THE GREATEST WRITERS THE WORLD
HAS EVER KNOWN.

HE WROTE COMEDIES, TRAGEDIES,
HISTORIES, AND ROMANCES ABOUT
ANCIENT HEROES, BLOODY WARS,
AND MAGICAL CREATURES.

THIS IS ONE OF THOSE STORIES . . .

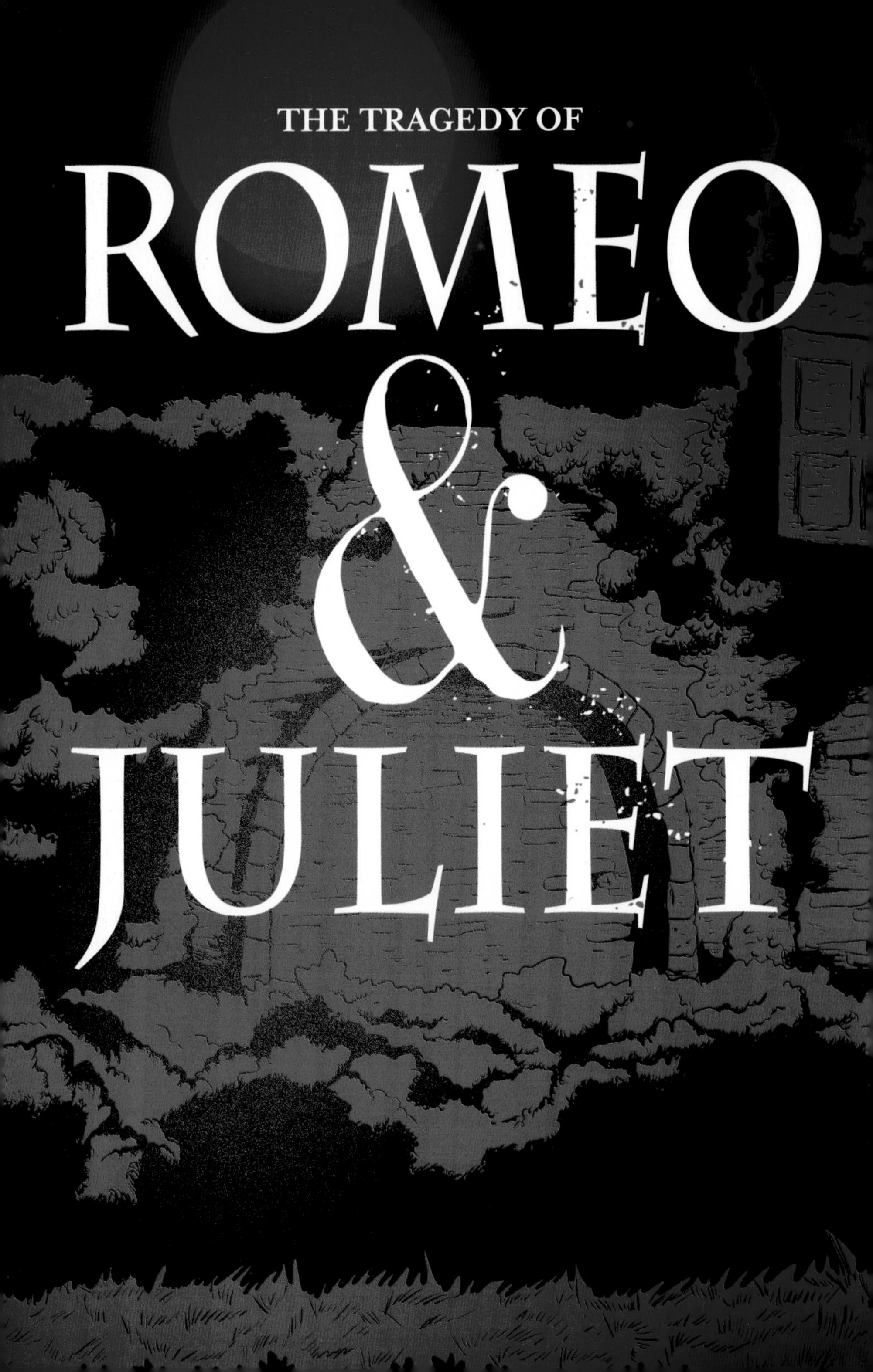
THE TRAGEDY OF
ROMEO
&
JULIET

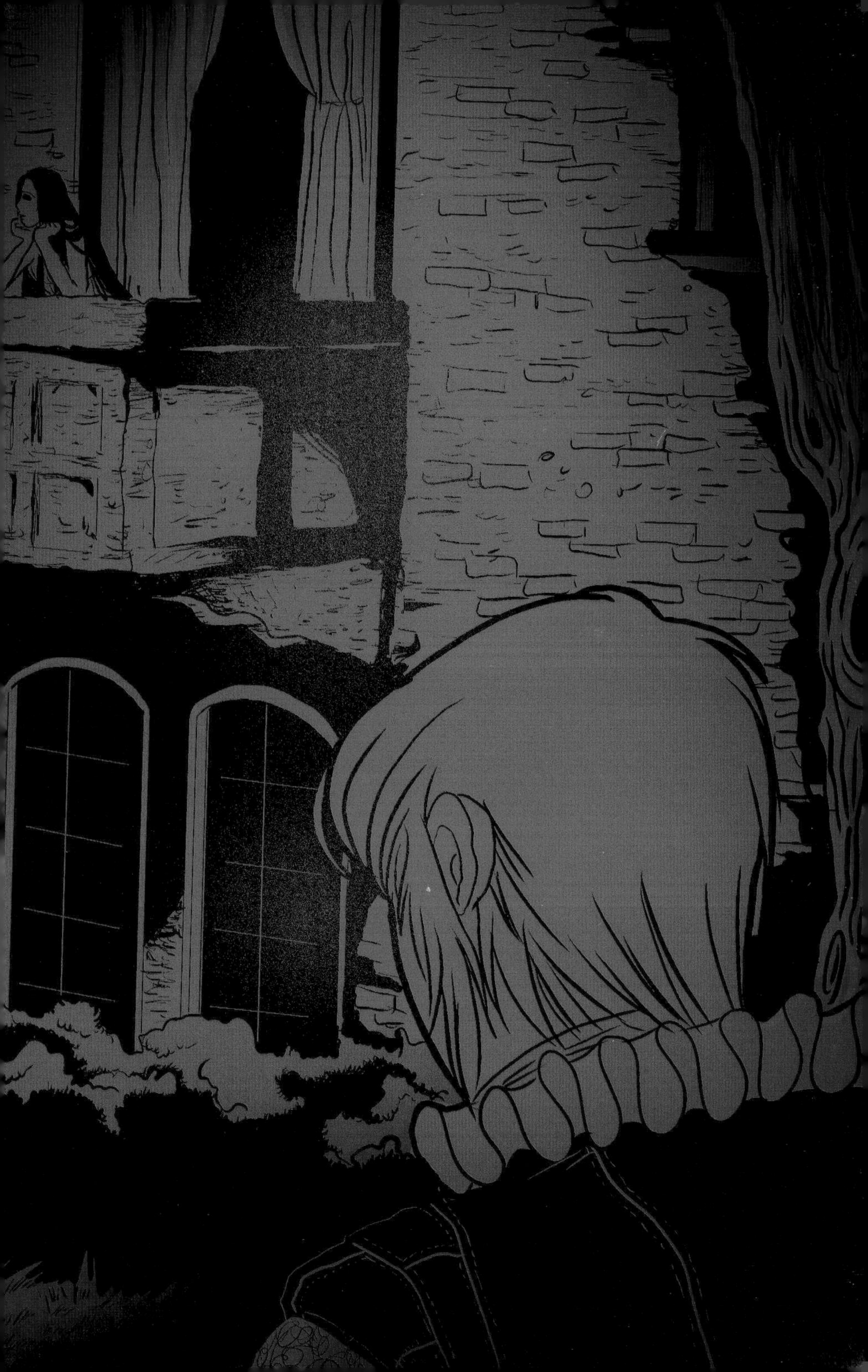

THE CAST

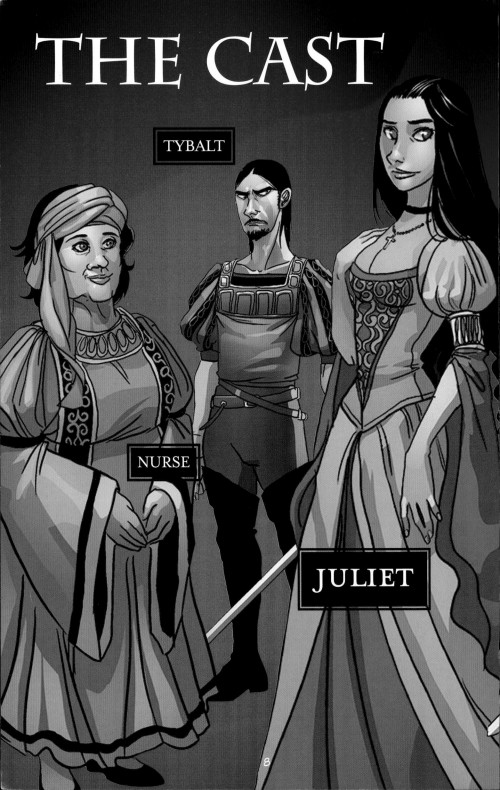

TYBALT

NURSE

JULIET

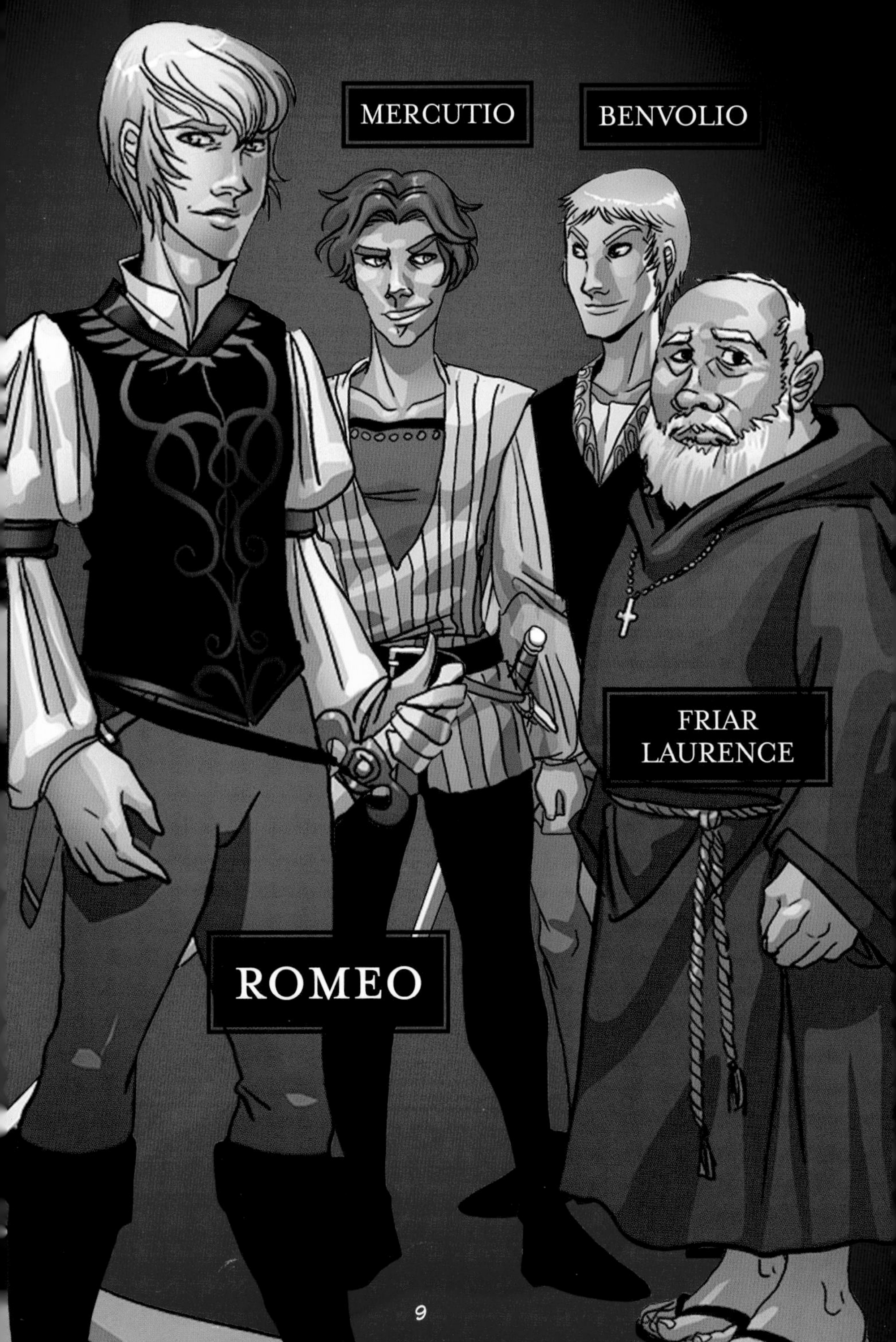
MERCUTIO
BENVOLIO
FRIAR LAURENCE
ROMEO

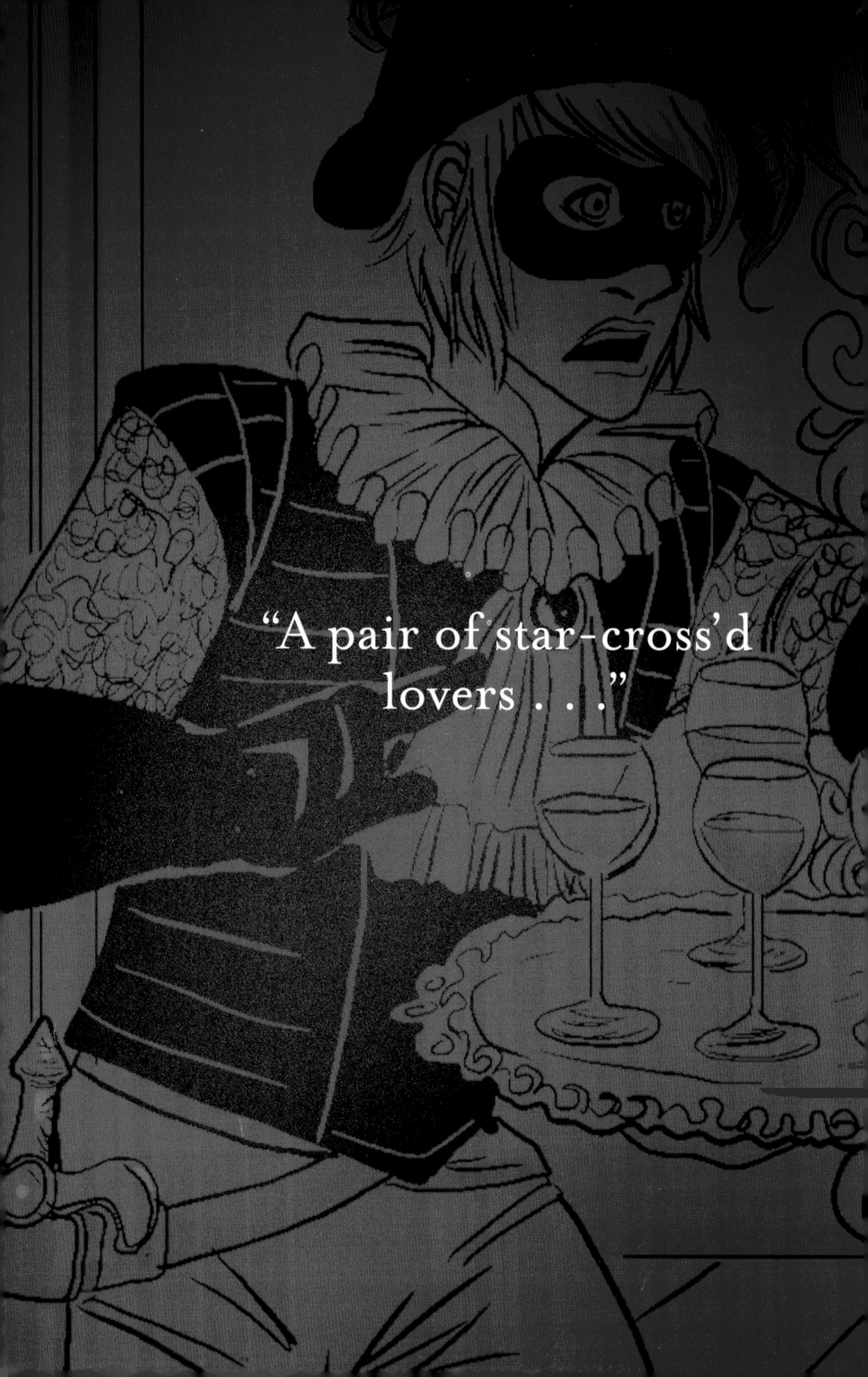

"A pair of star-cross'd lovers . . ."

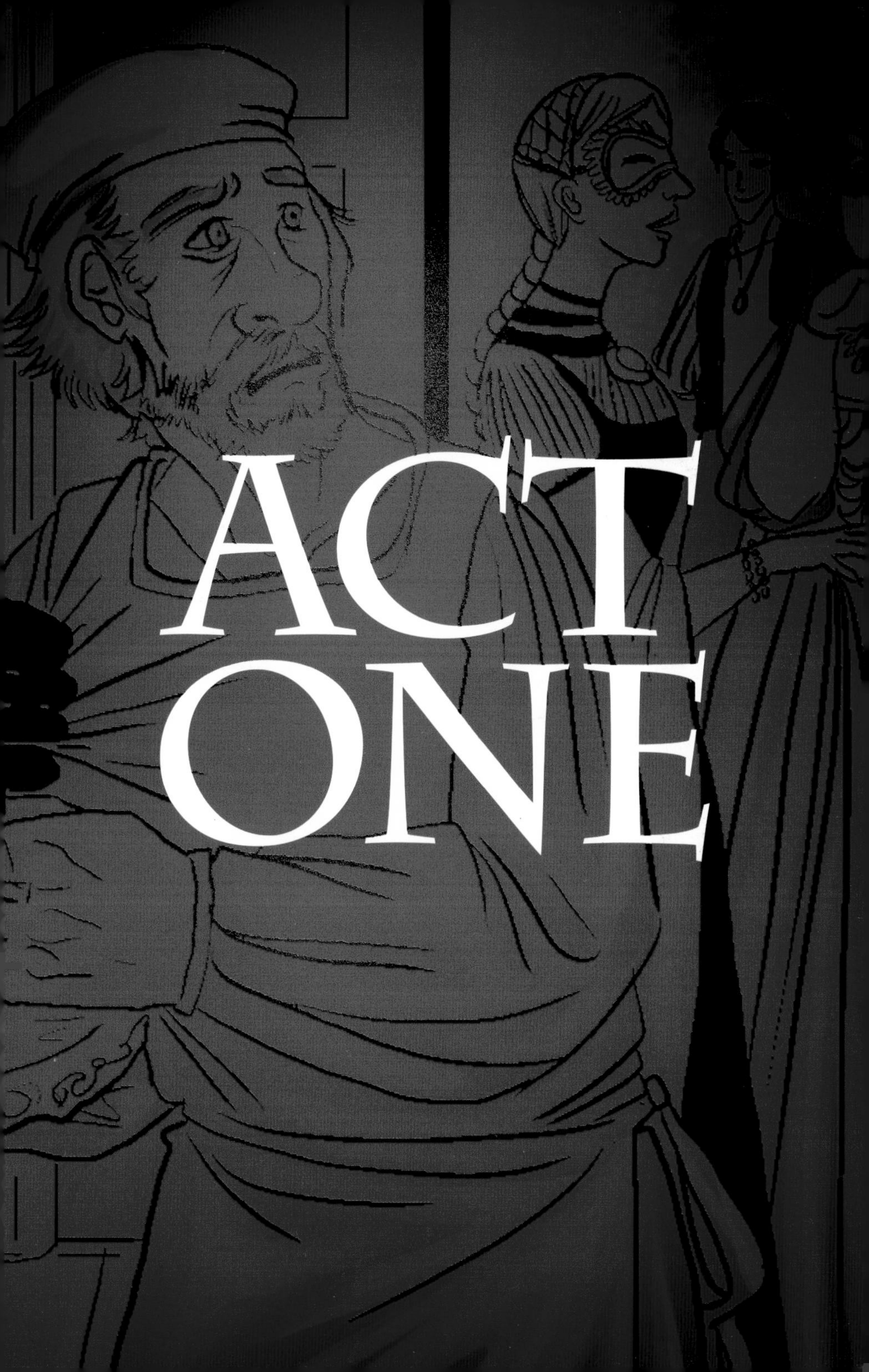

ACT ONE

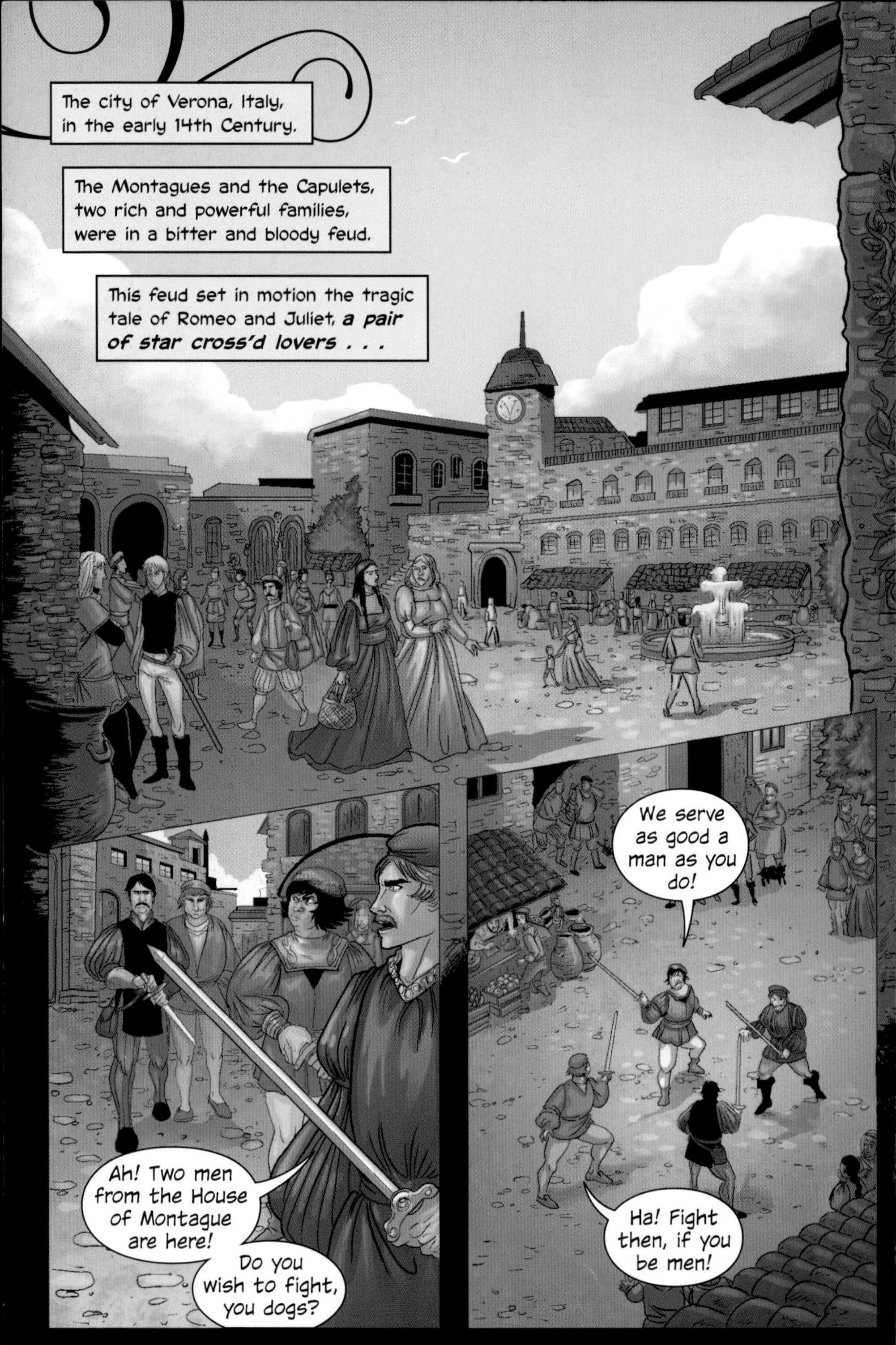
The city of Verona, Italy, in the early 14th Century.
The Montagues and the Capulets, two rich and powerful families, were in a bitter and bloody feud.
This feud set in motion the tragic tale of Romeo and Juliet, ***a pair of star cross'd lovers . . .***
Ah! Two men from the House of Montague are here!
Do you wish to fight, you dogs?
We serve as good a man as you do!
Ha! Fight then, if you be men!

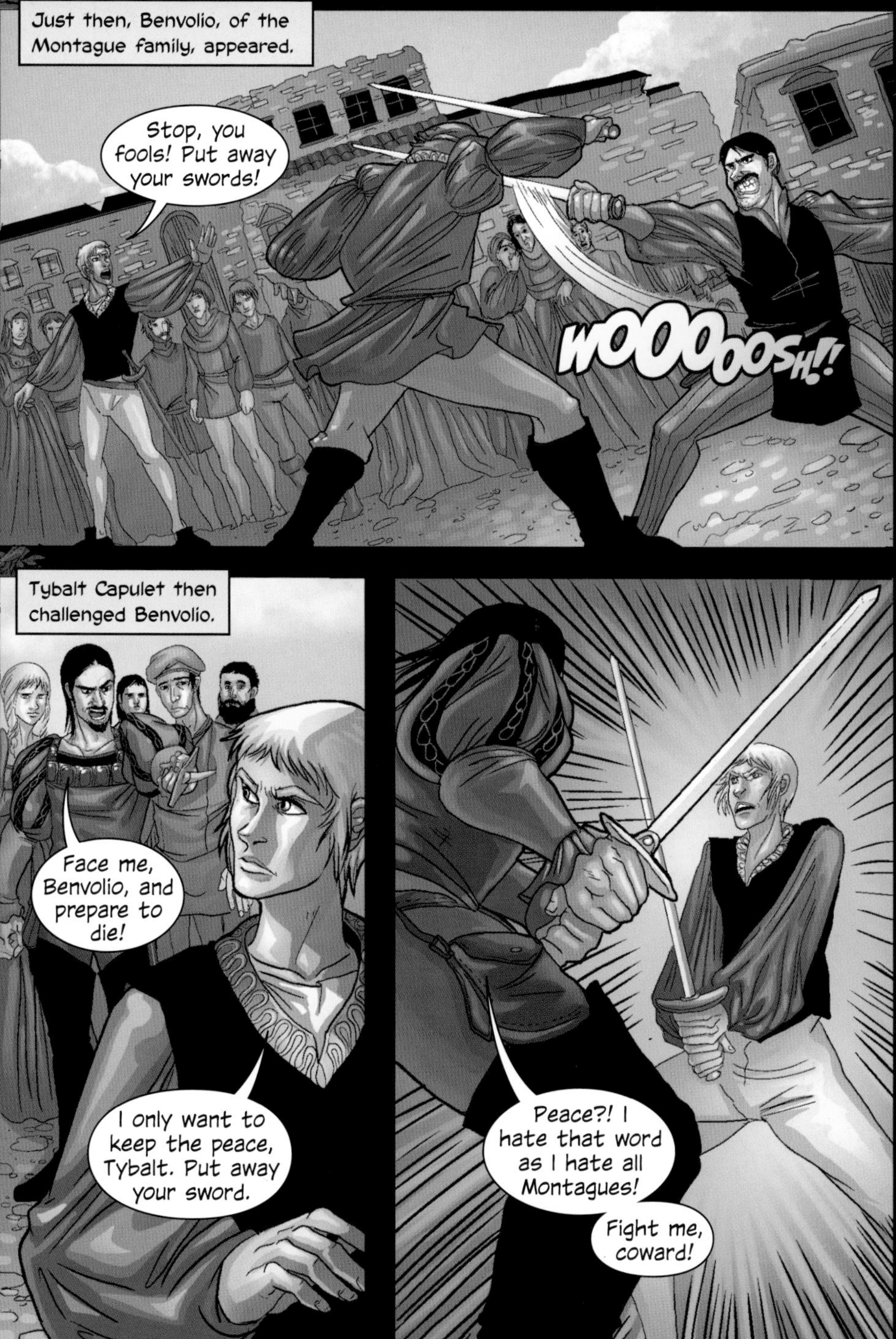
Just then, Benvolio, of the Montague family, appeared.
Stop, you fools! Put away your swords!
WOOOOOSH!!
Tybalt Capulet then challenged Benvolio.
Face me, Benvolio, and prepare to die!
I only want to keep the peace, Tybalt. Put away your sword.
Peace?! I hate that word as I hate all Montagues!
Fight me, coward!

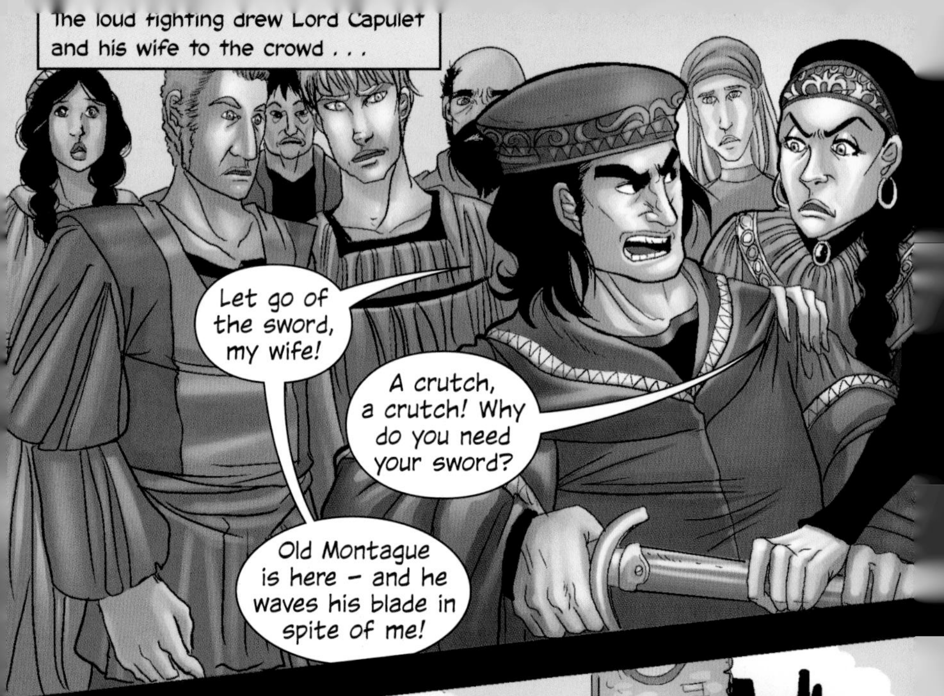
The loud fighting drew Lord Capulet and his wife to the crowd . . .
Let go of the sword, my wife!
A crutch, a crutch! Why do you need your sword?
Old Montague is here – and he waves his blade in spite of me!

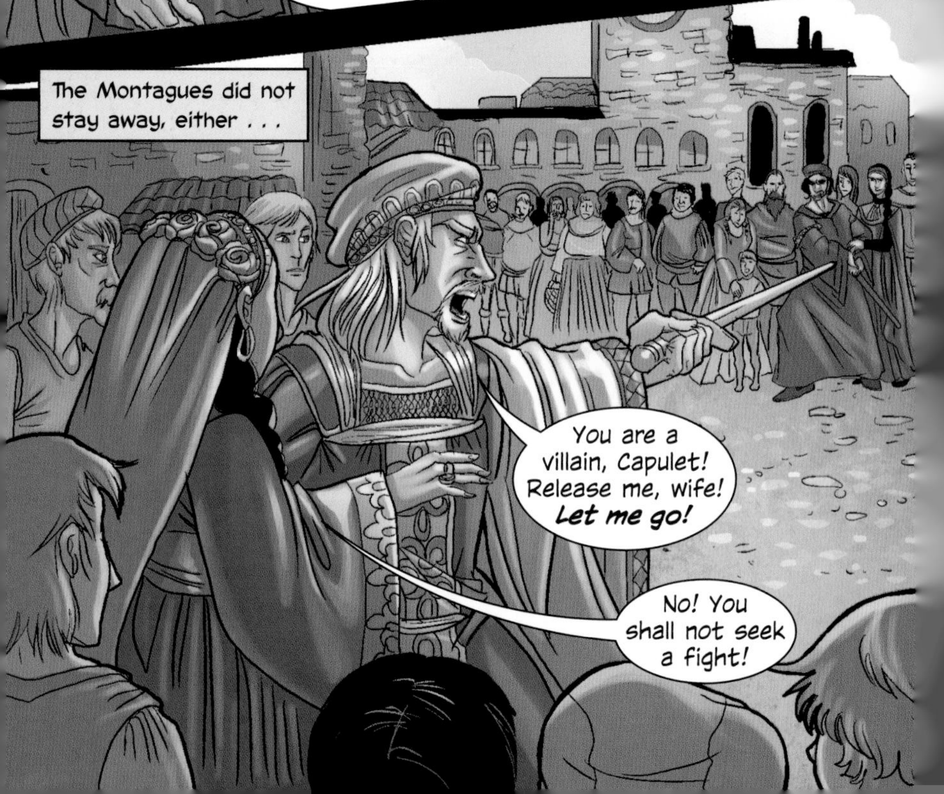
The Montagues did not stay away, either . . .
You are a villain, Capulet! Release me, wife! Let me go!
No! You shall not seek a fight!

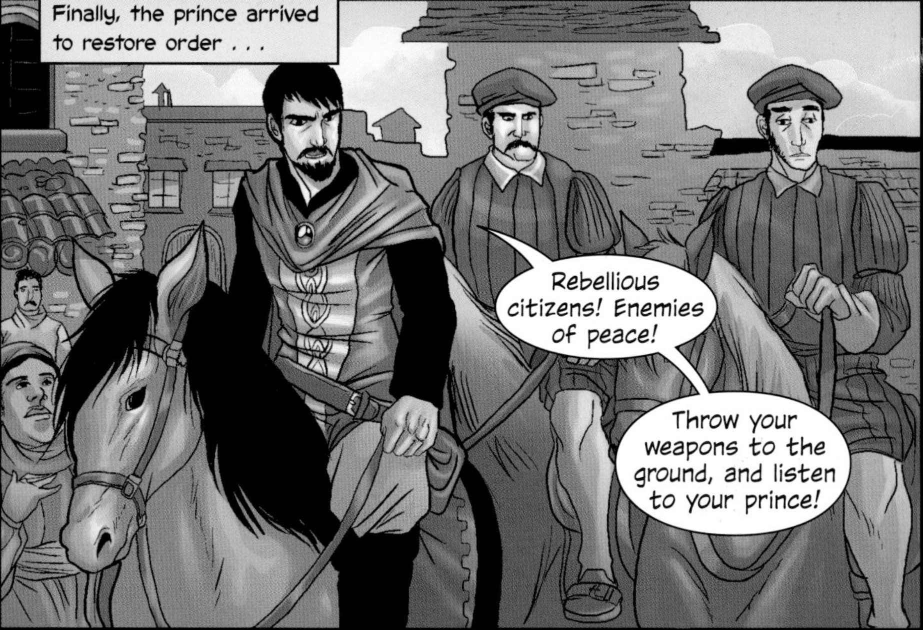
Finally, the prince arrived to restore order . . .
Rebellious citizens! Enemies of peace!
Throw your weapons to the ground, and listen to your prince!

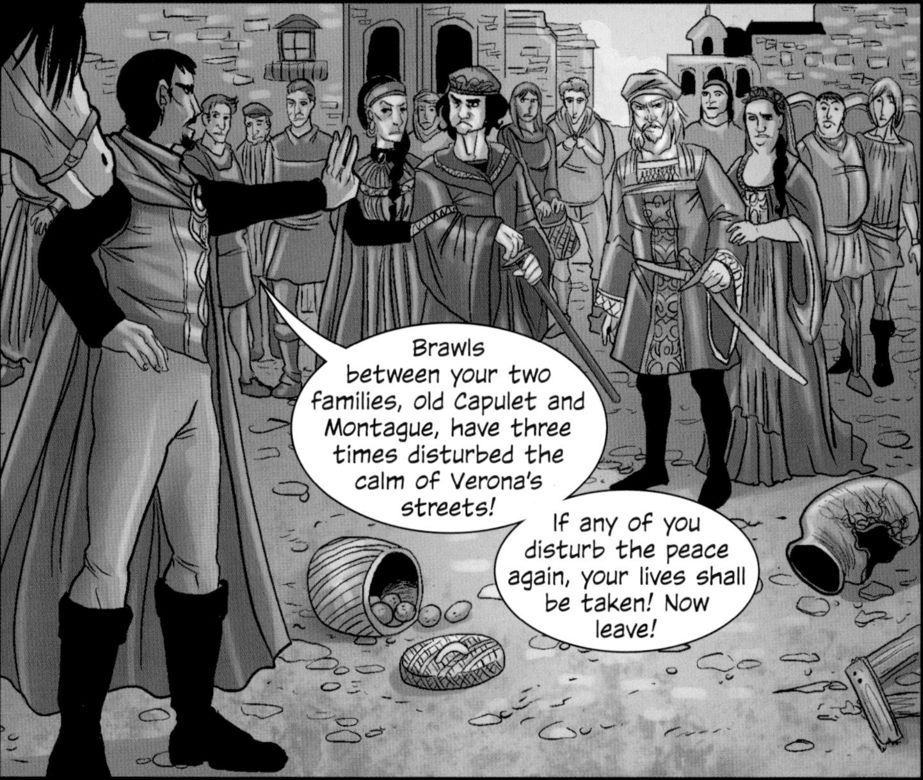
Brawls between your two families, old Capulet and Montague, have three times disturbed the calm of Verona's streets!
If any of you disturb the peace again, your lives shall be taken! Now leave!

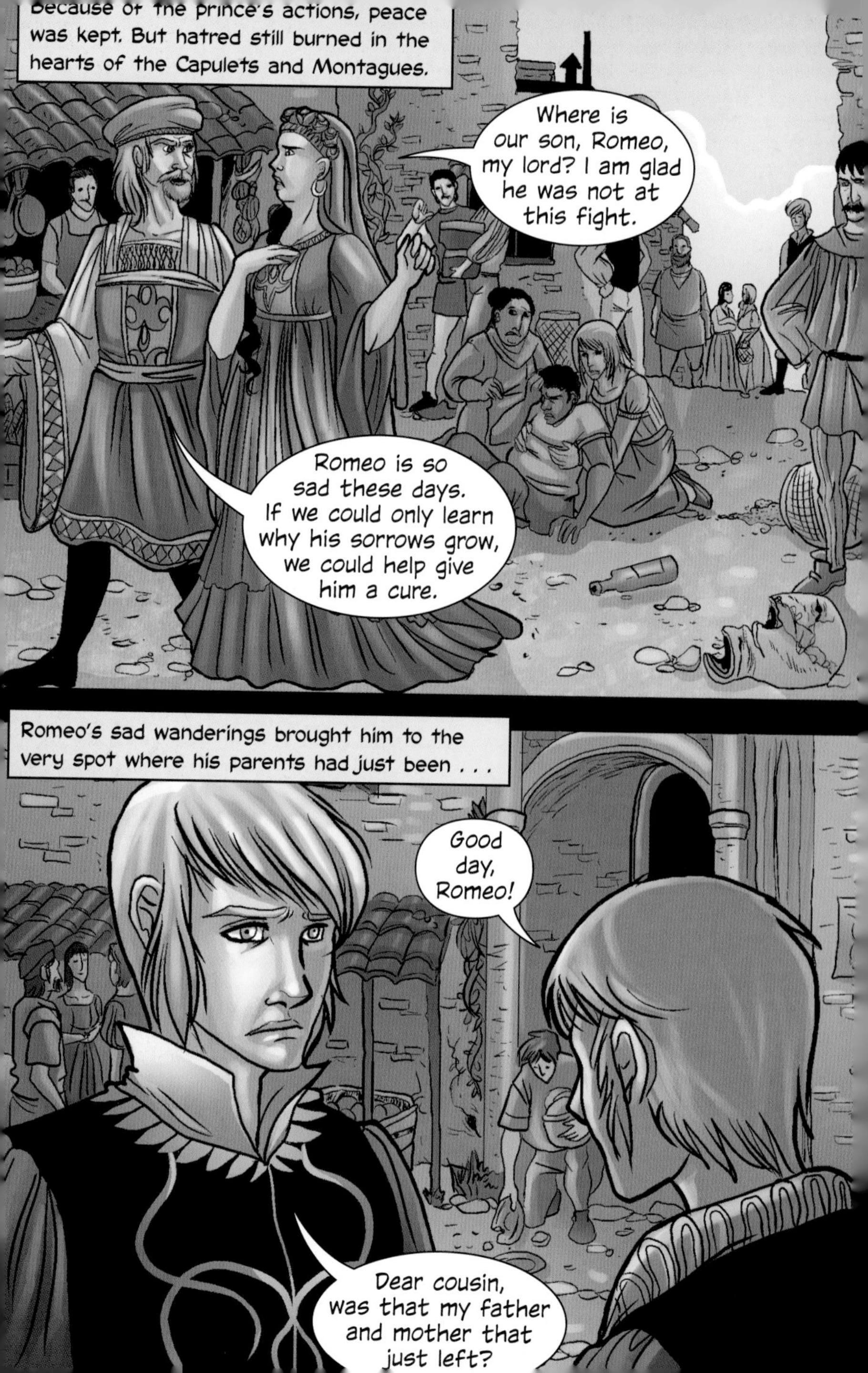
Because of the prince's actions, peace was kept. But hatred still burned in the hearts of the Capulets and Montagues.
Where is our son, Romeo, my lord? I am glad he was not at this fight.
Romeo is so sad these days. If we could only learn why his sorrows grow, we could help give him a cure.
Romeo's sad wanderings brought him to the very spot where his parents had just been . . .
Good day, Romeo!
Dear cousin, was that my father and mother that just left?

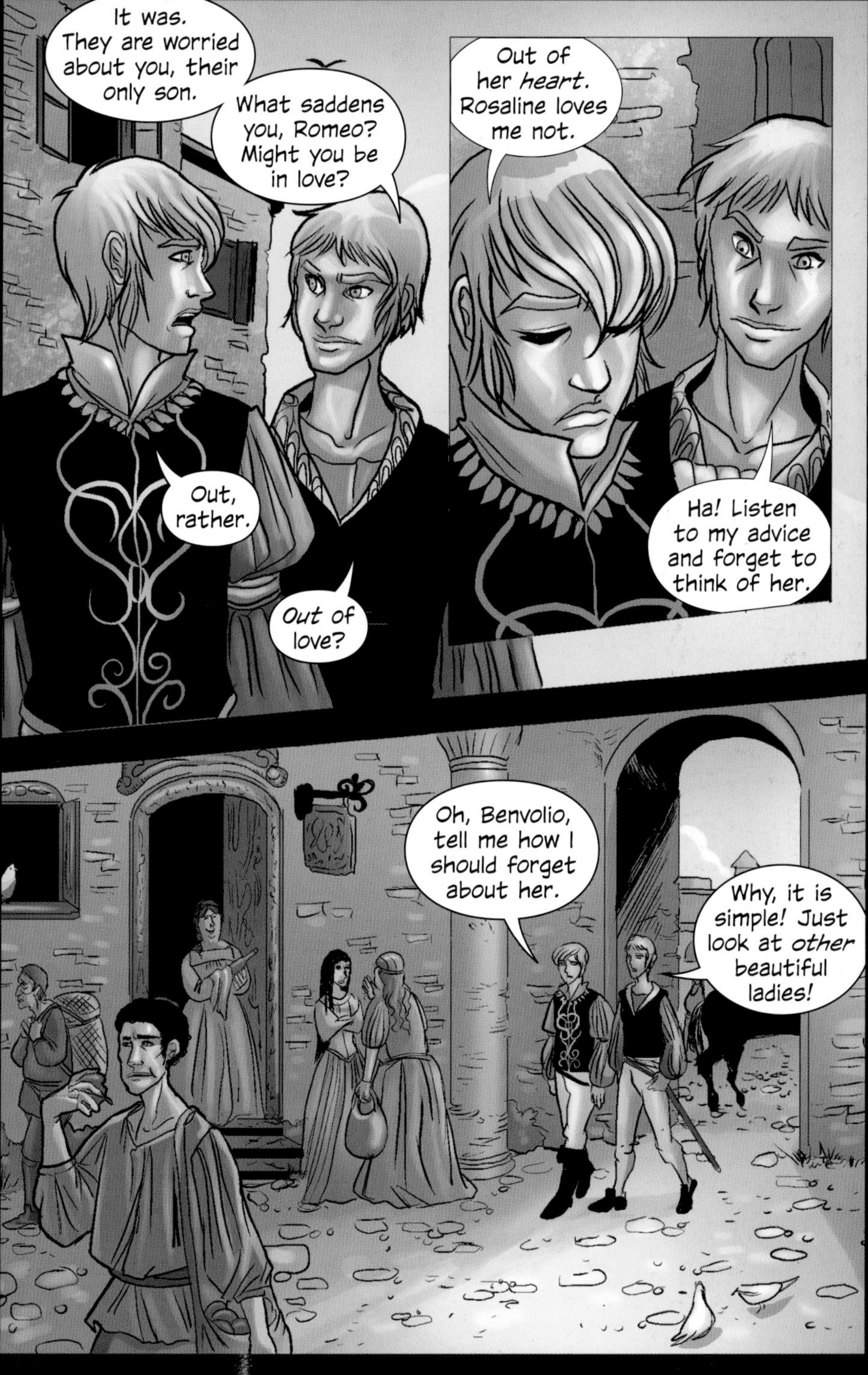
It was. They are worried about you, their only son.
What saddens you, Romeo? Might you be in love?
Out, rather.
Out of love?
Out of her heart. Rosaline loves me not.
Ha! Listen to my advice and forget to think of her.
Oh, Benvolio, tell me how I should forget about her.
Why, it is simple! Just look at other beautiful ladies!

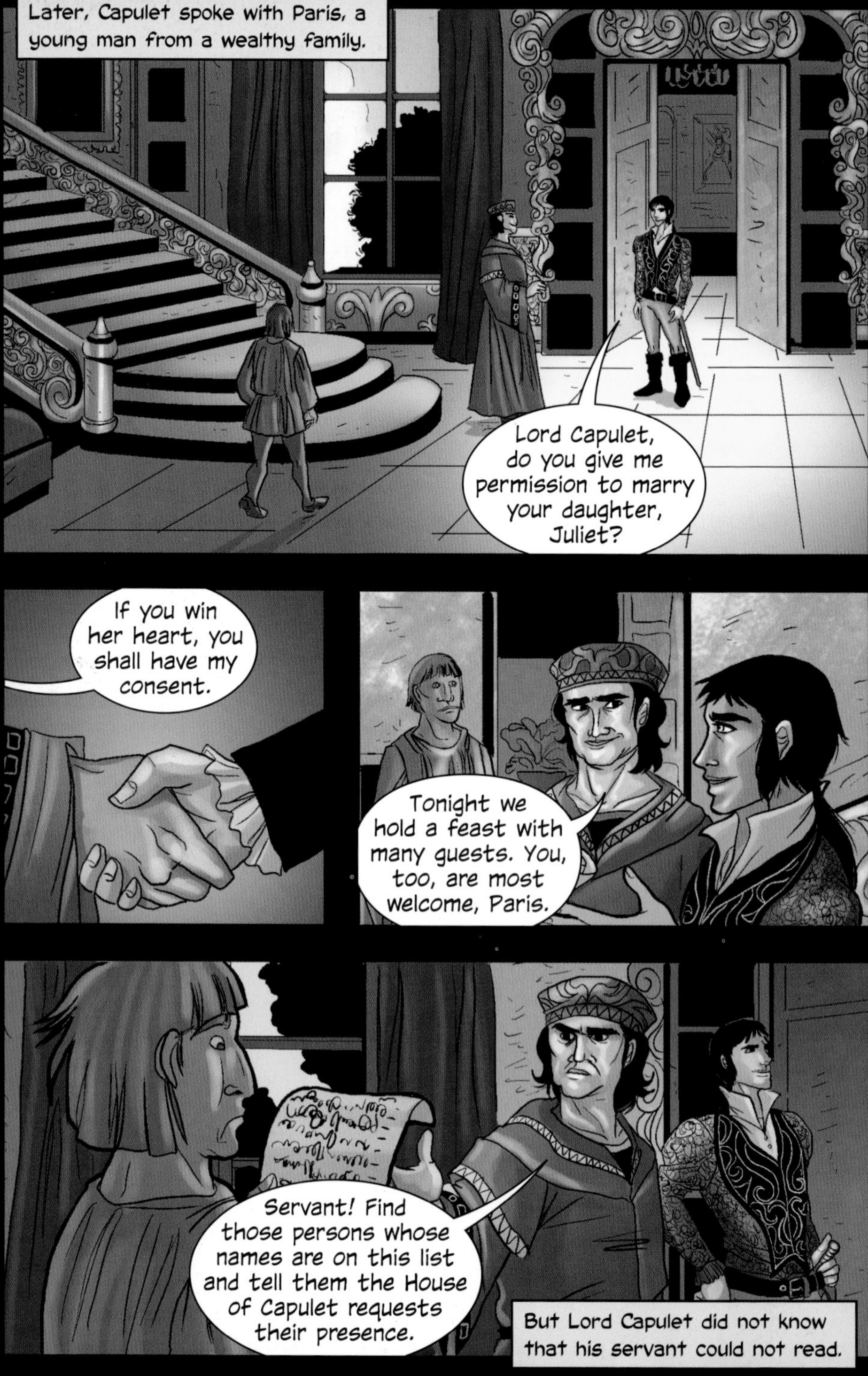
Later, Capulet spoke with Paris, a young man from a wealthy family.
Lord Capulet, do you give me permission to marry your daughter, Juliet?
If you win her heart, you shall have my consent.
Tonight we hold a feast with many guests. You, too, are most welcome, Paris.
Servant! Find those persons whose names are on this list and tell them the House of Capulet requests their presence.
But Lord Capulet did not know that his servant could not read.

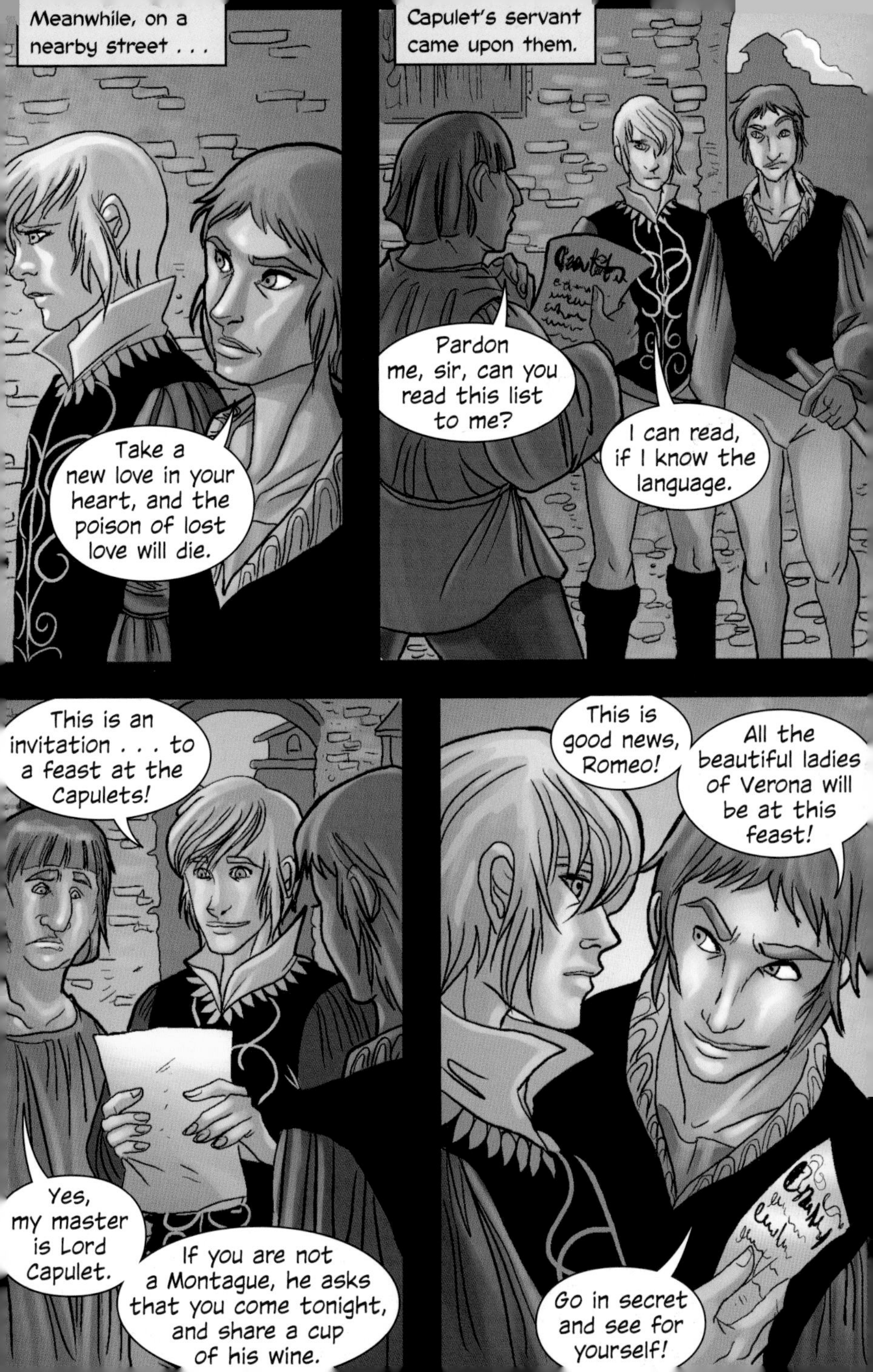
Meanwhile, on a nearby street . . .
Take a new love in your heart, and the poison of lost love will die.
Capulet's servant came upon them.
Pardon me, sir, can you read this list to me?
I can read, if I know the language.
This is an invitation . . . to a feast at the Capulets!
Yes, my master is Lord Capulet.
If you are not a Montague, he asks that you come tonight, and share a cup of his wine.
This is good news, Romeo!
All the beautiful ladies of Verona will be at this feast!
Go in secret and see for yourself!

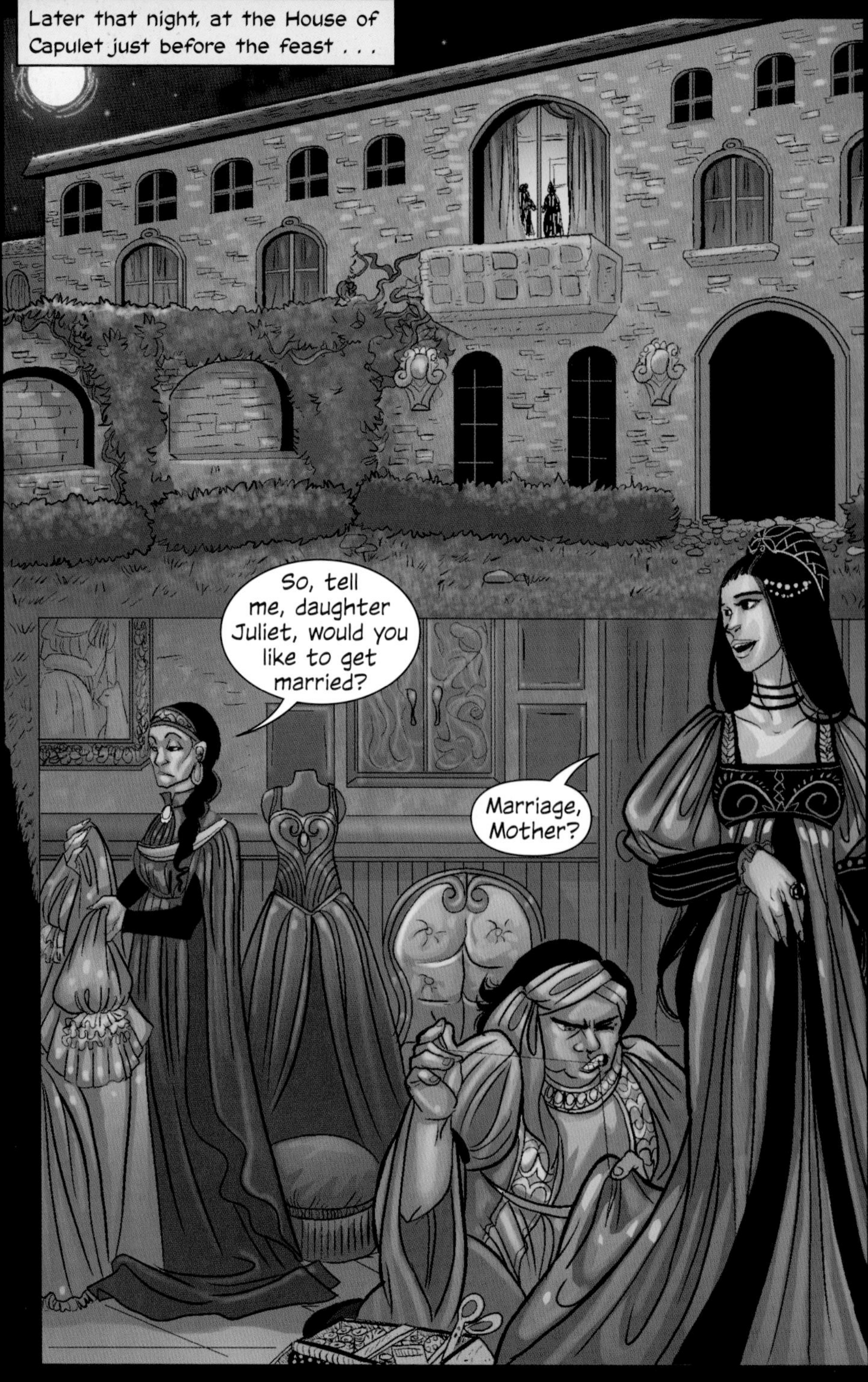
Later that night, at the House of Capulet just before the feast . . .
So, tell me, daughter Juliet, would you like to get married?
Marriage, Mother?

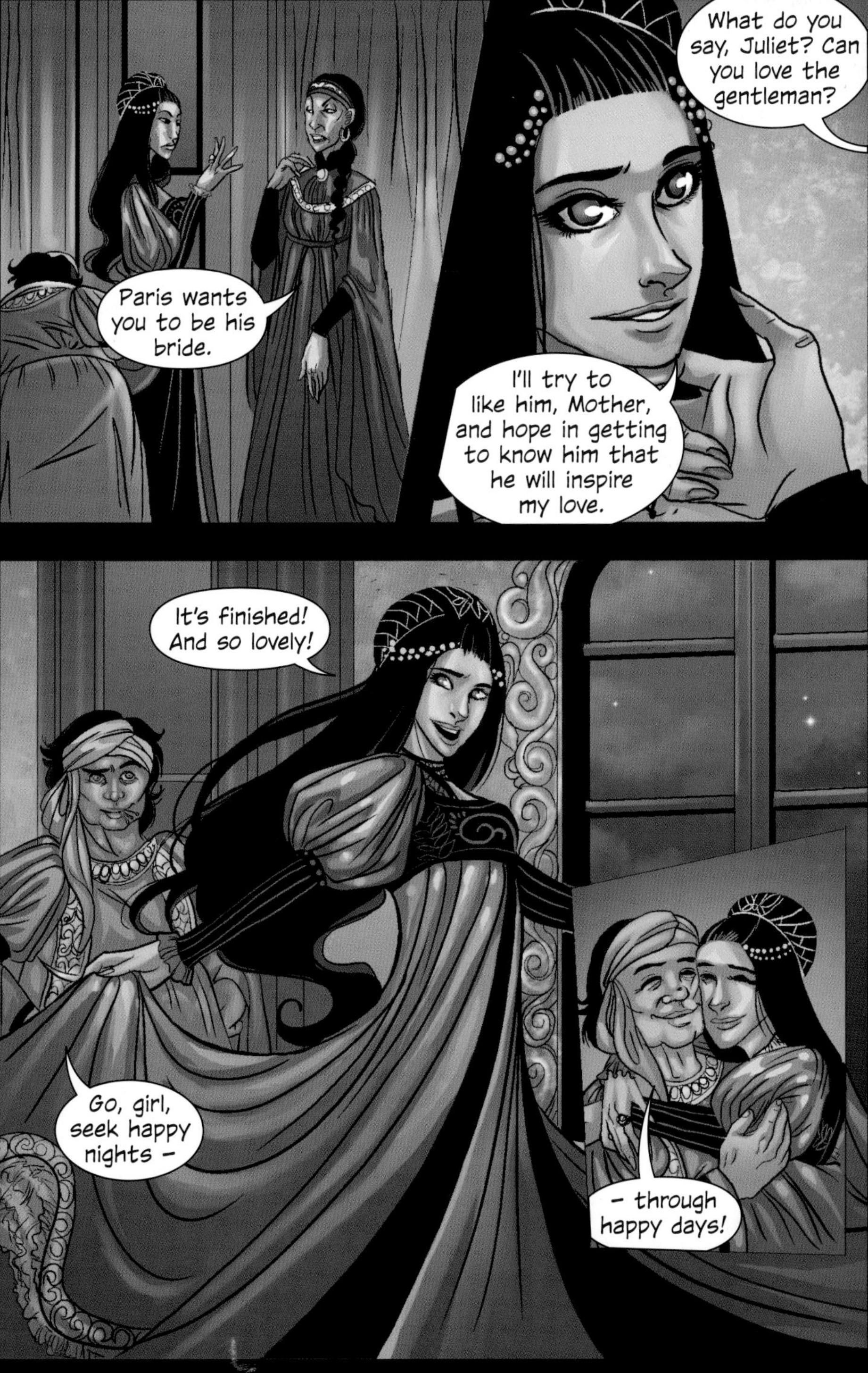
Paris wants you to be his bride.
What do you say, Juliet? Can you love the gentleman?
I'll try to like him, Mother, and hope in getting to know him that he will inspire my love.
It's finished! And so lovely!
Go, girl, seek happy nights –
– through happy days!

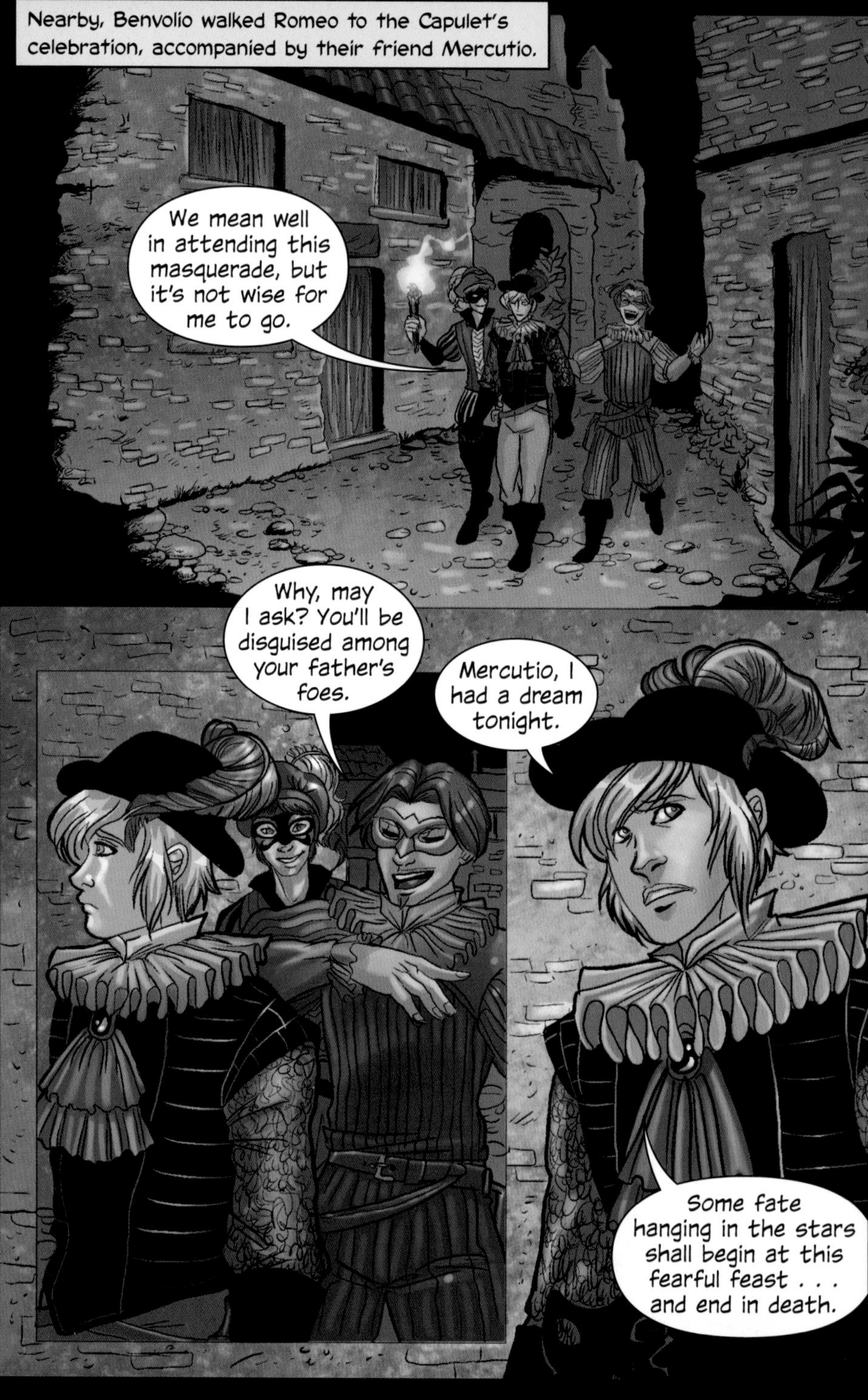
Nearby, Benvolio walked Romeo to the Capulet's celebration, accompanied by their friend Mercutio.
We mean well in attending this masquerade, but it's not wise for me to go.
Why, may I ask? You'll be disguised among your father's foes.
Mercutio, I had a dream tonight.
Some fate hanging in the stars shall begin at this fearful feast . . . and end in death.

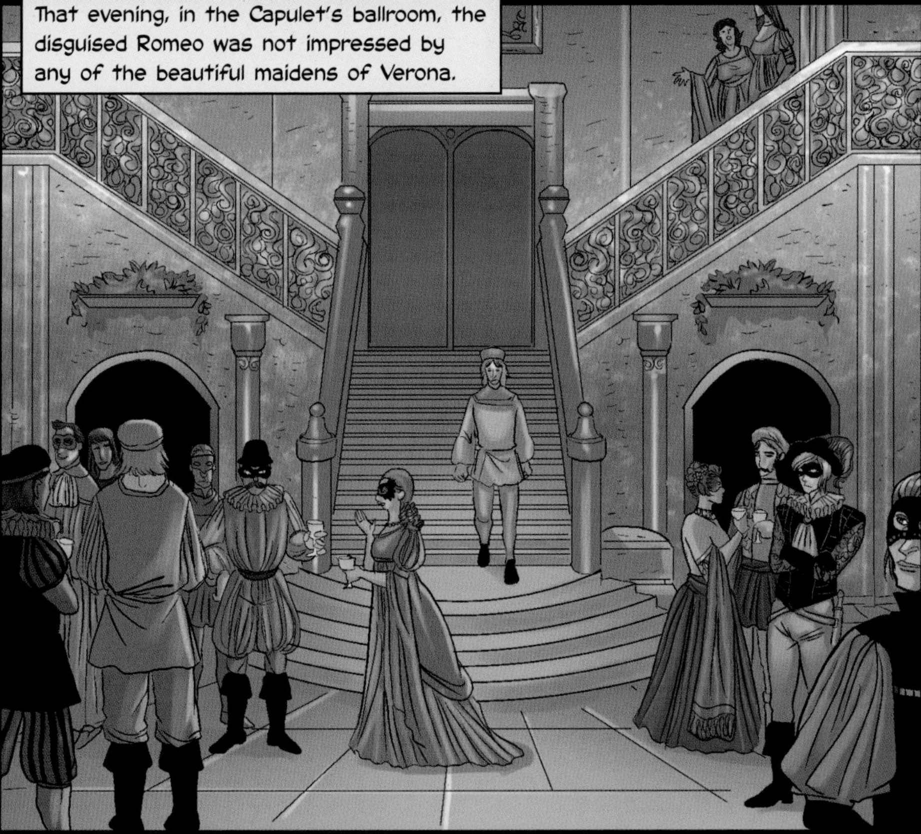
That evening, in the Capulet's ballroom, the disguised Romeo was not impressed by any of the beautiful maidens of Verona.

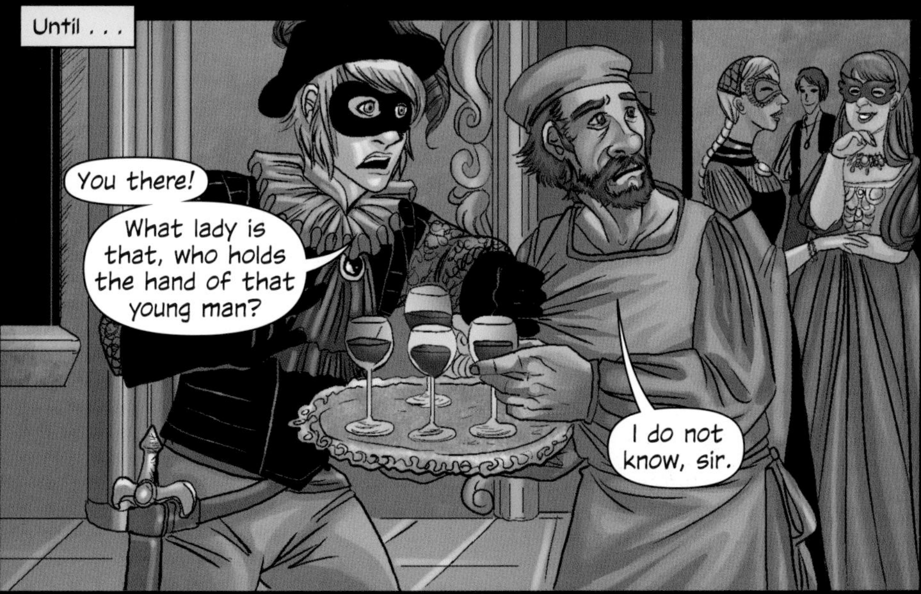
Until . . .
You there!
What lady is that, who holds the hand of that young man?
I do not know, sir.

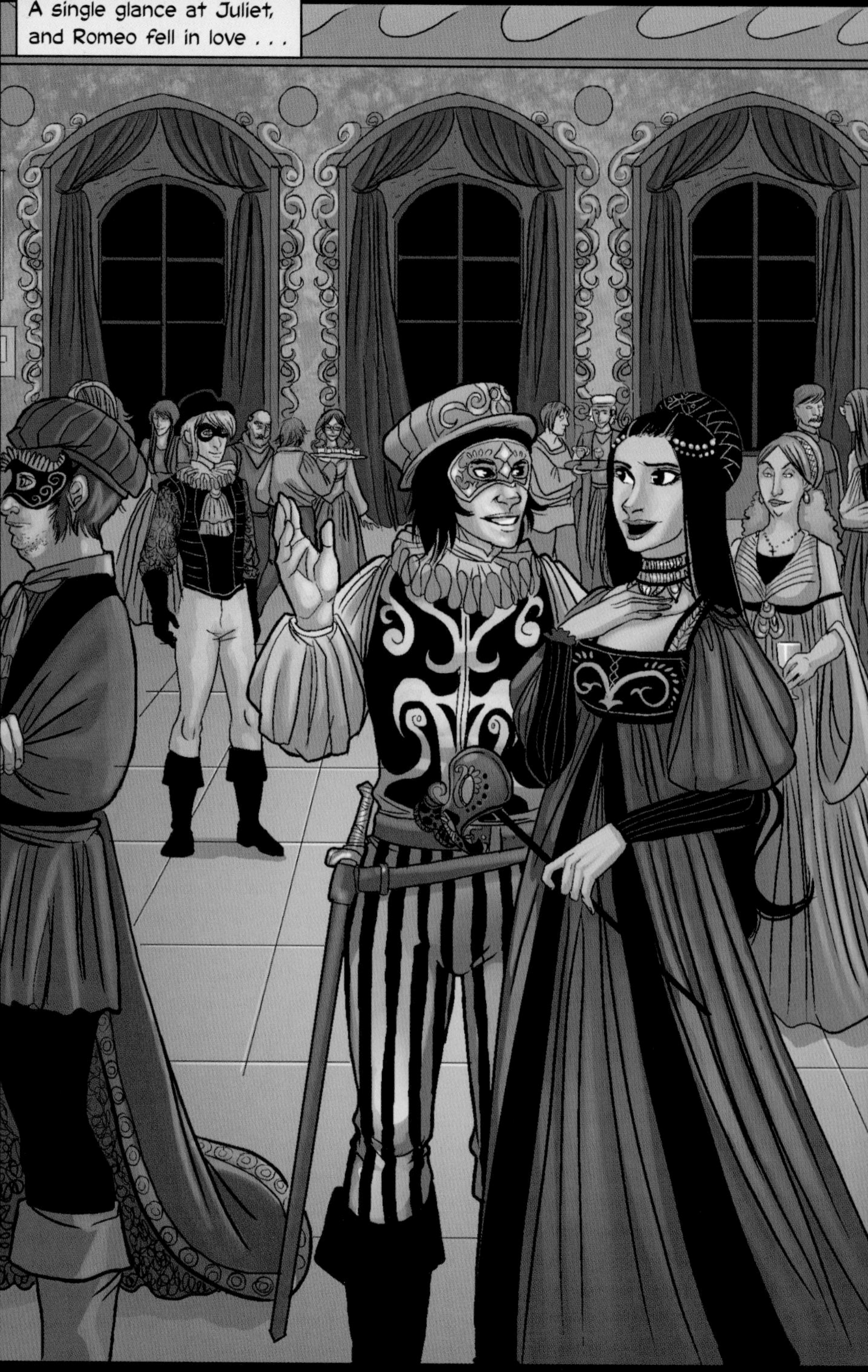
A single glance at Juliet, and Romeo fell in love . . .

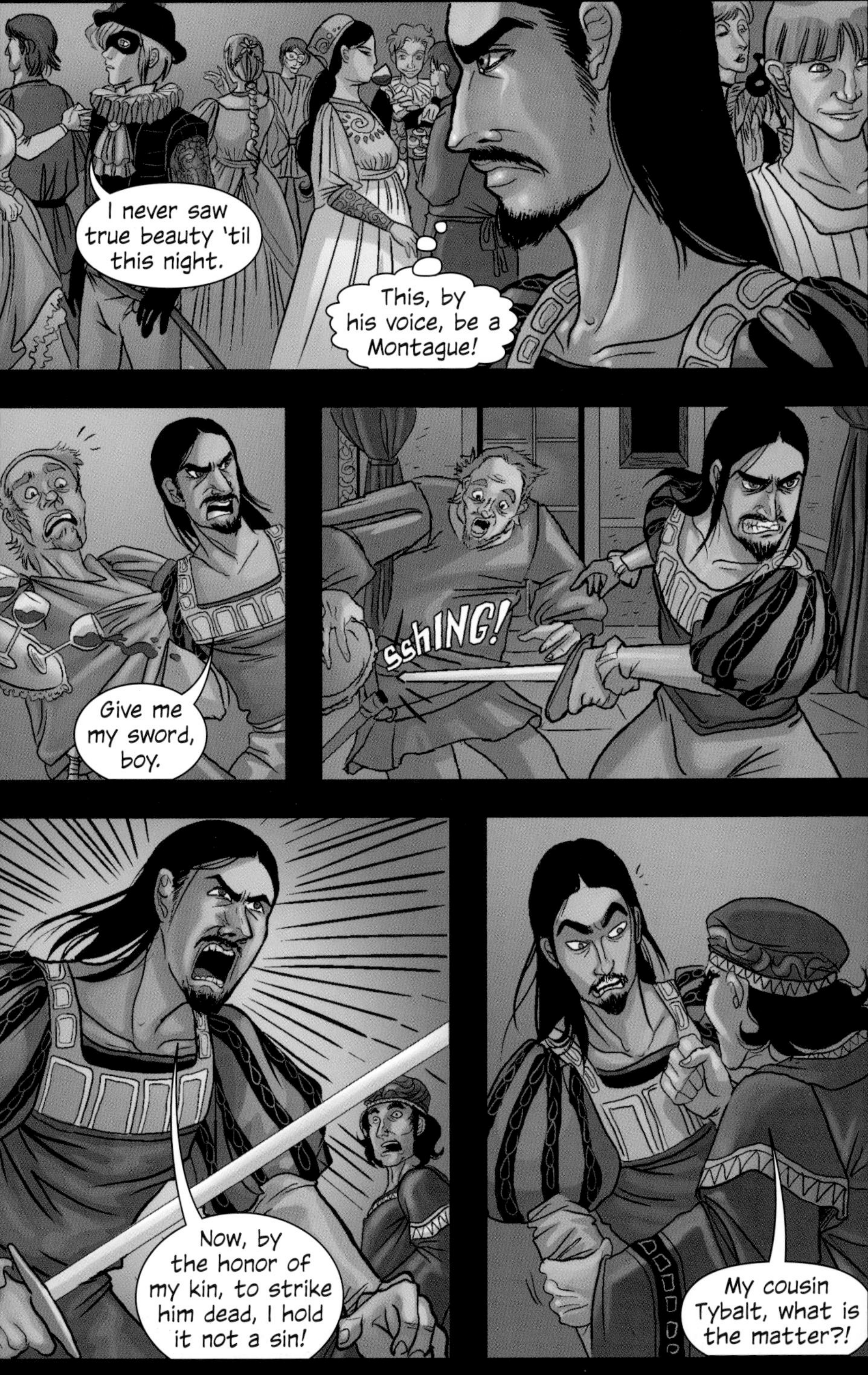
I never saw true beauty 'til this night.
This, by his voice, be a Montague!
Give me my sword, boy.
sshING!
Now, by the honor of my kin, to strike him dead, I hold it not a sin!
My cousin Tybalt, what is the matter?!

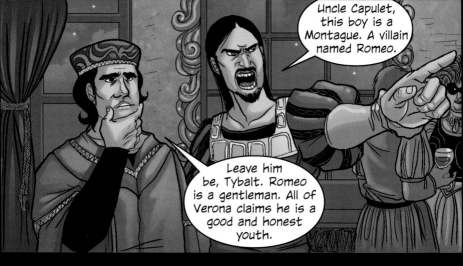

Uncle Capulet, this boy is a Montague. A villain named Romeo.

Leave him be, Tybalt. Romeo is a gentleman. All of Verona claims he is a good and honest youth.

Besides, I would not allow a fight in my own house. We must keep the prince's peace.

He should not be here!

Am I the master of this house, or are you?

As you command, my lord, but this will lead to our misfortune.

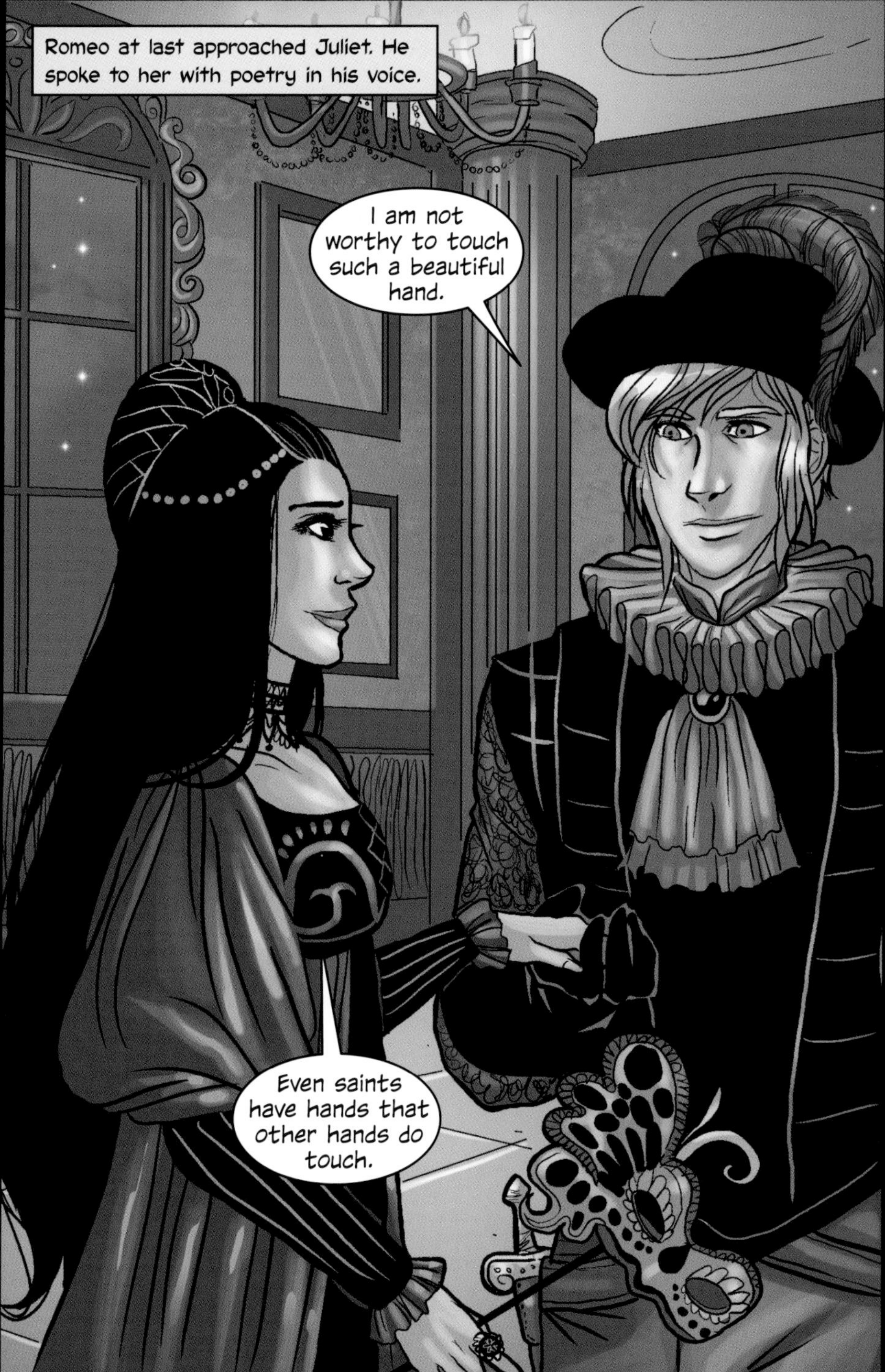
Romeo at last approached Juliet. He spoke to her with poetry in his voice.
I am not worthy to touch such a beautiful hand.
Even saints have hands that other hands do touch.

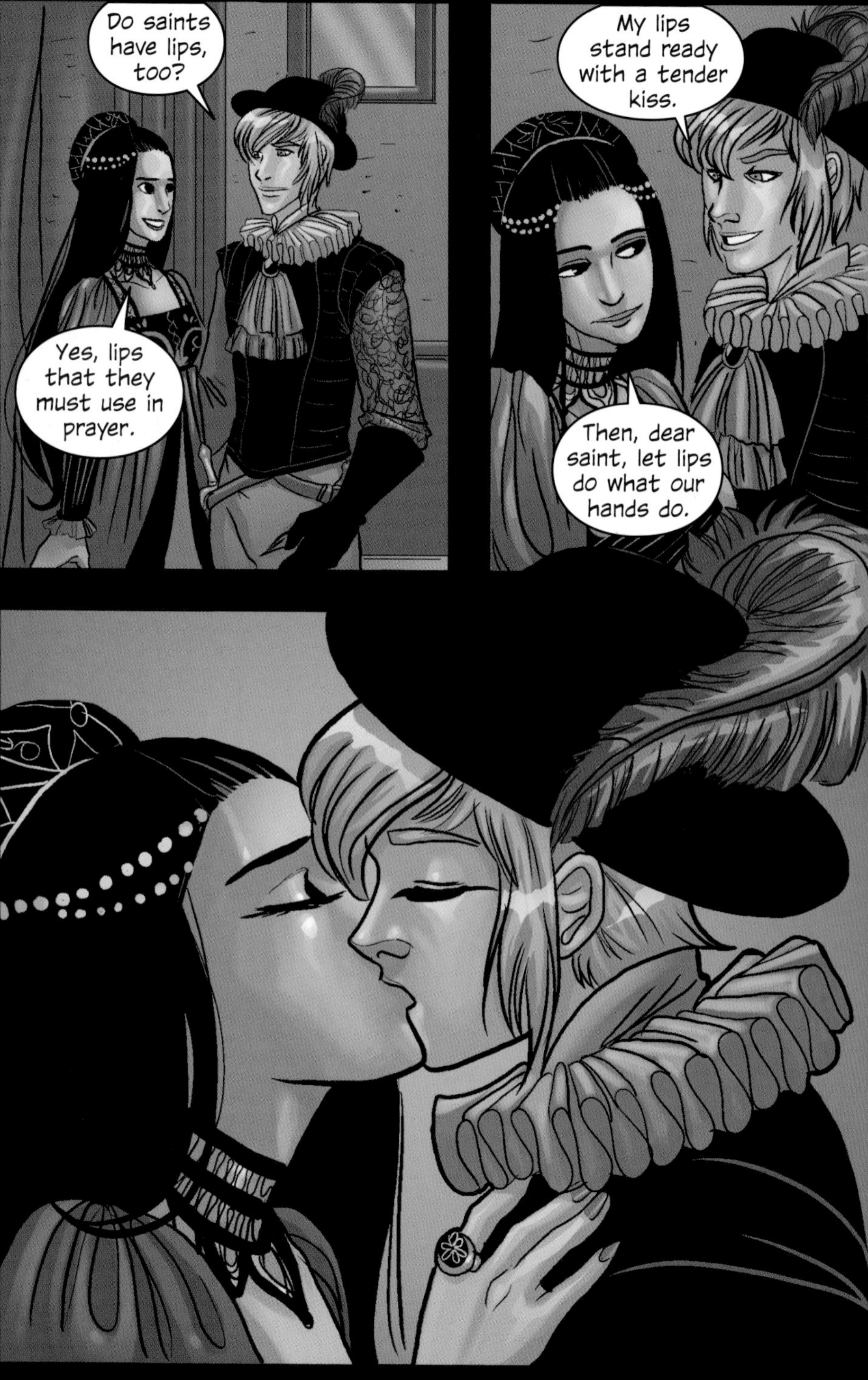
Do saints have lips, too?
Yes, lips that they must use in prayer.
My lips stand ready with a tender kiss.
Then, dear saint, let lips do what our hands do.

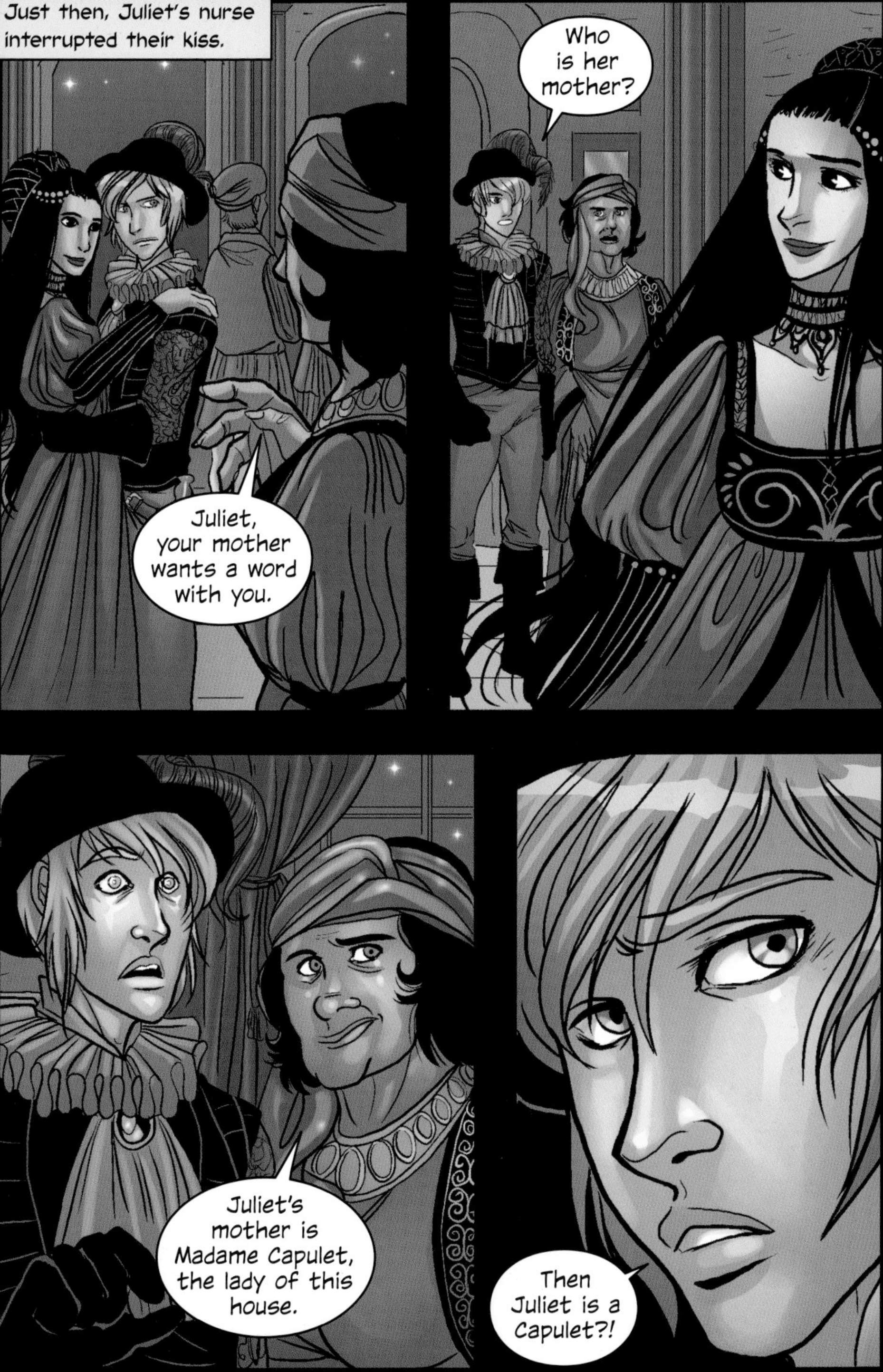
Just then, Juliet's nurse interrupted their kiss.
Juliet, your mother wants a word with you.
Who is her mother?
Juliet's mother is Madame Capulet, the lady of this house.
Then Juliet is a Capulet?!

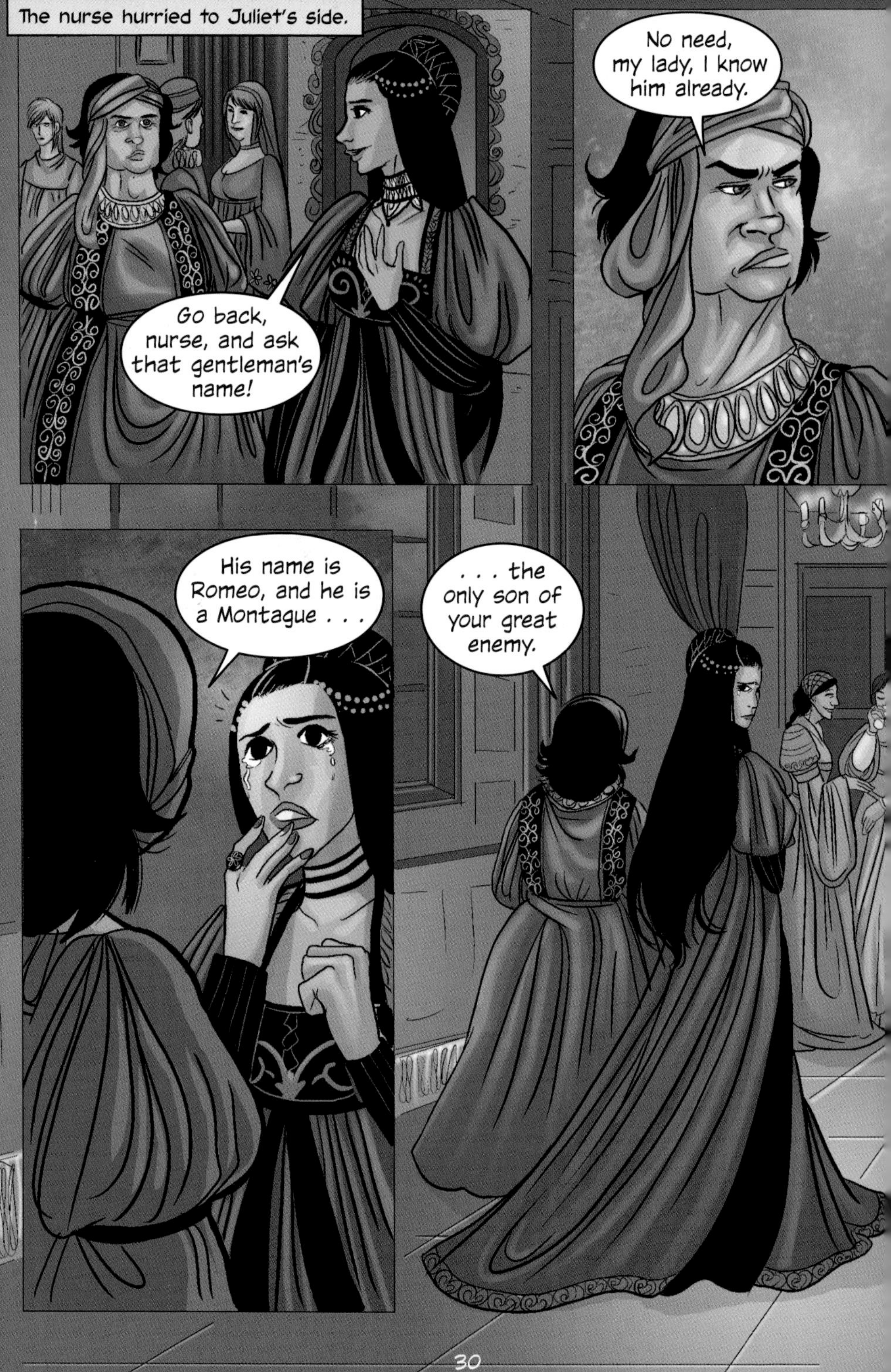
The nurse hurried to Juliet's side.
Go back, nurse, and ask that gentleman's name!
No need, my lady, I know him already.
His name is Romeo, and he is a Montague . . .
. . . the only son of your great enemy.

Romeo returned to the Capulet home later that night.

He ran this way. Call for him, good Mercutio.

Romeo! Madman! Lover!

He is gone.

Come, Benvolio, let us go.

In the shadows of the Capulet house, Romeo waited . . .

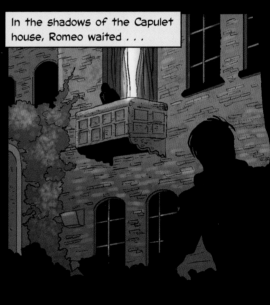

. . . and watched.

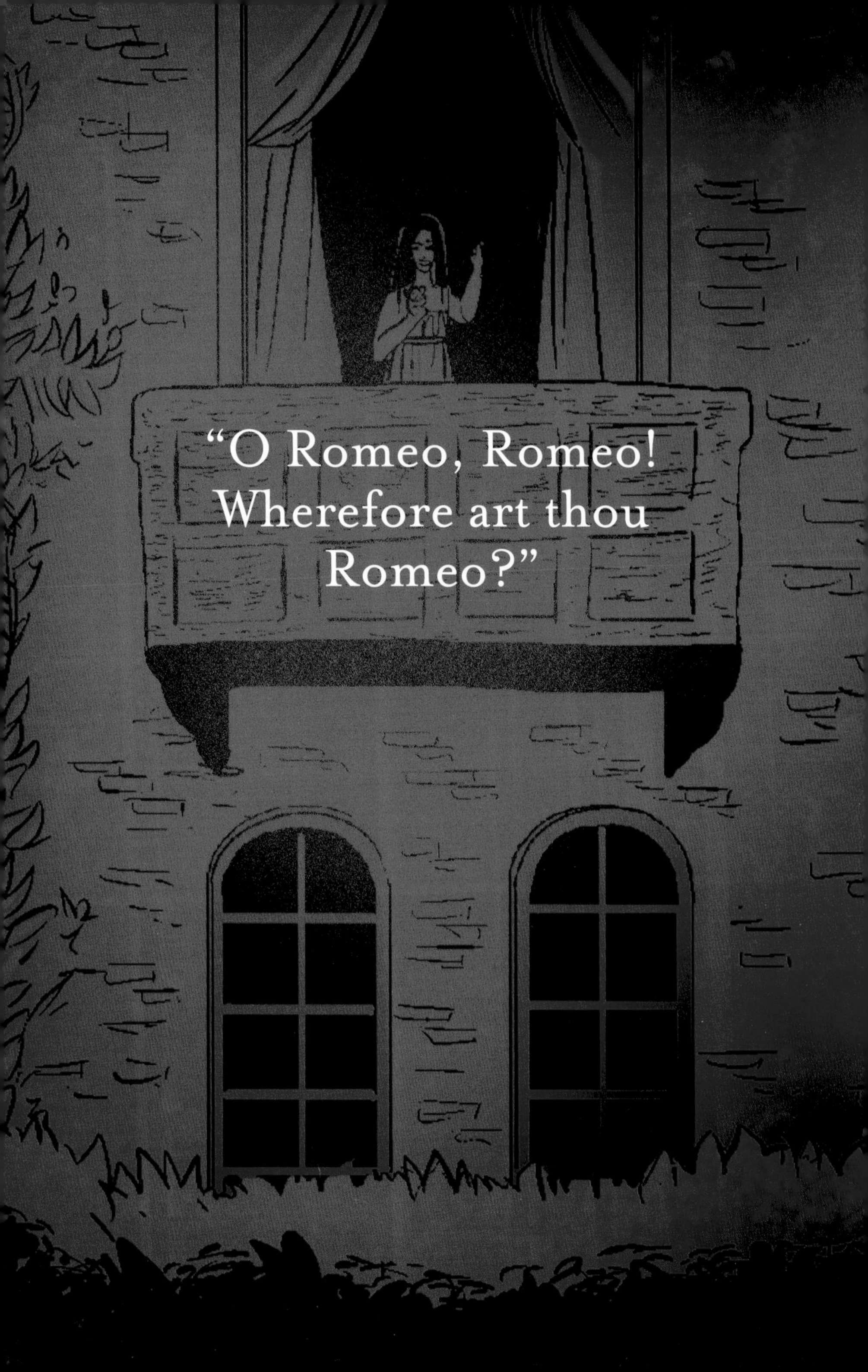
"O Romeo, Romeo! Wherefore art thou Romeo?"

ACT TWO

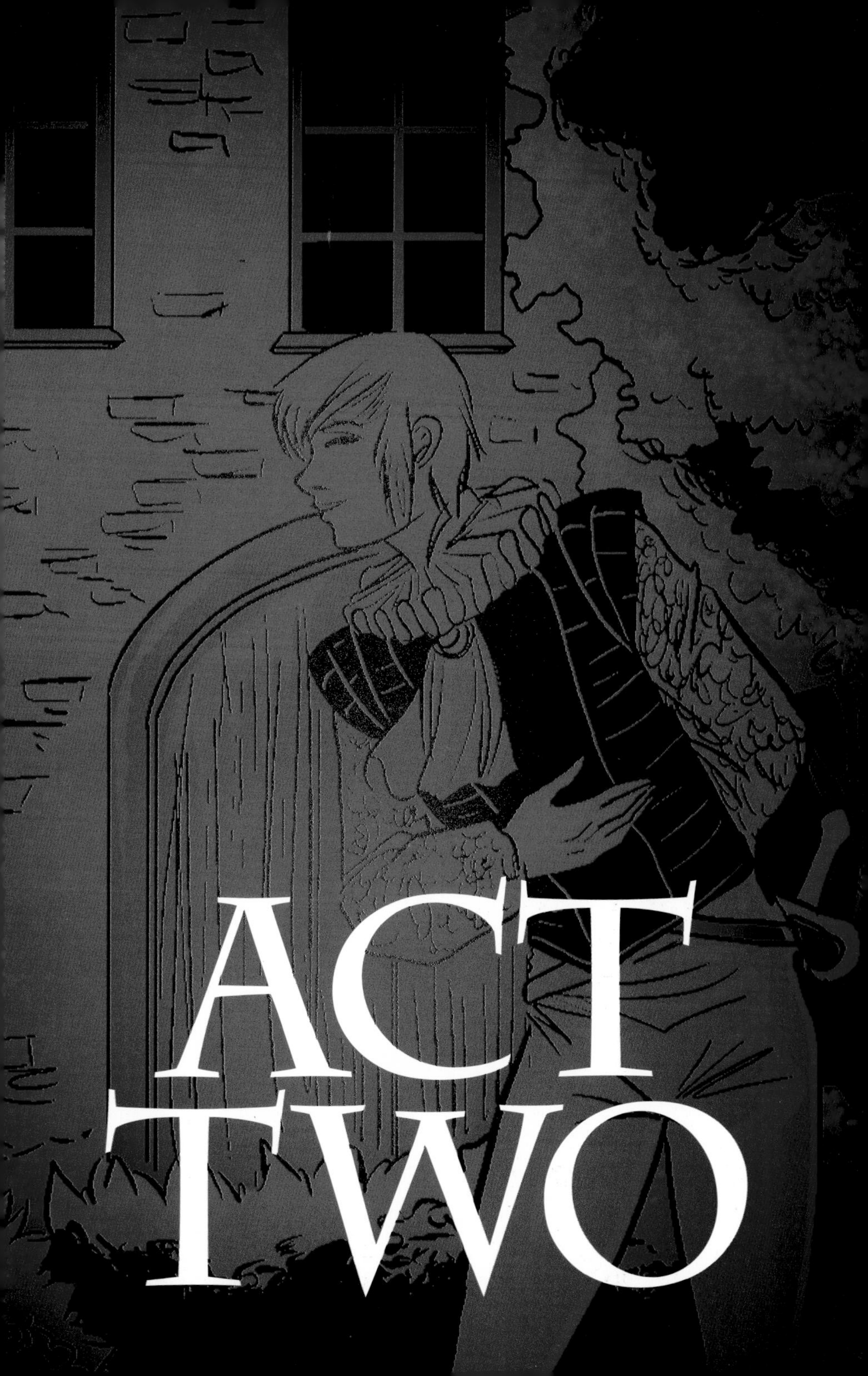

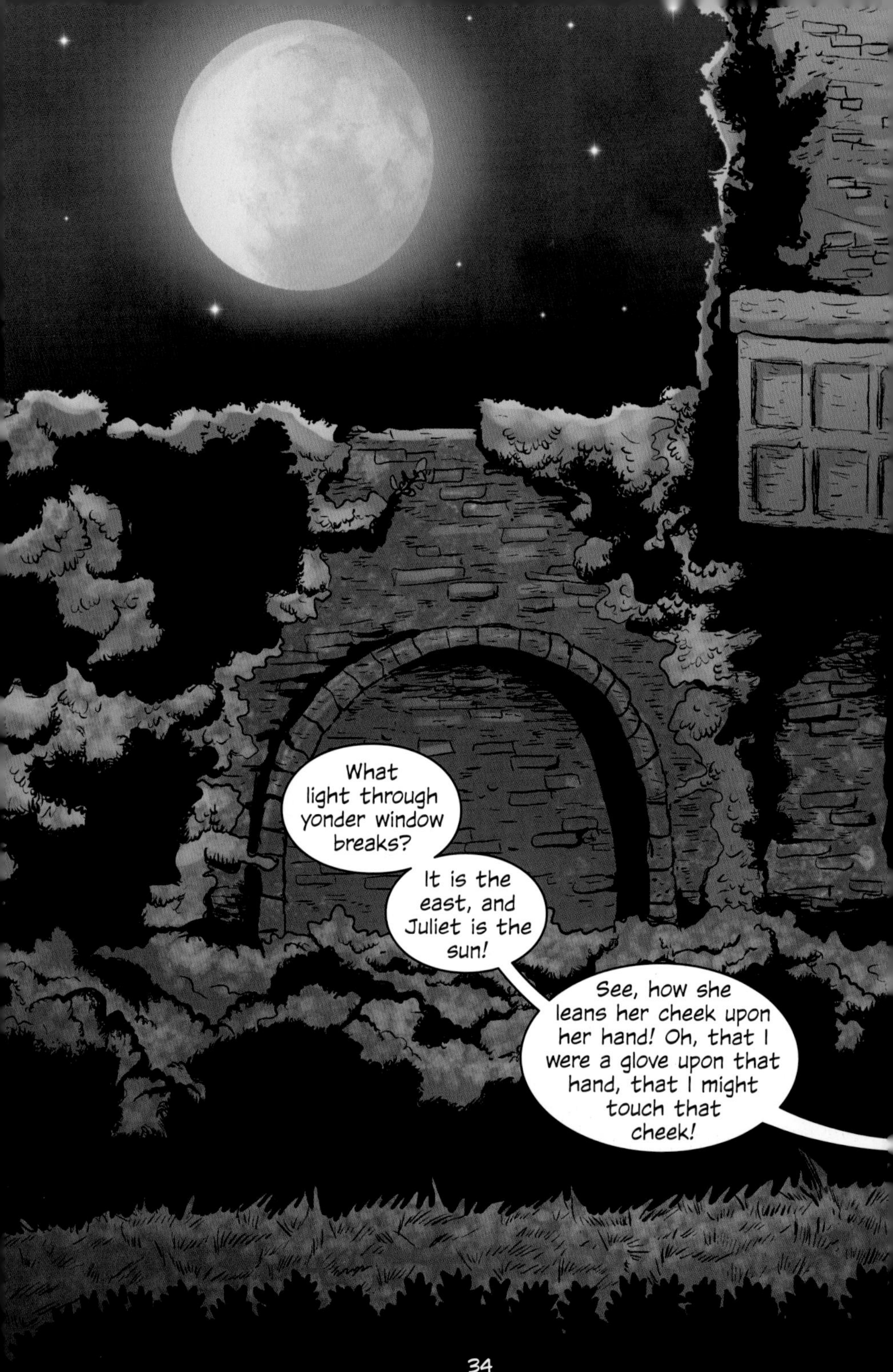
What light through yonder window breaks?
It is the east, and Juliet is the sun!
See, how she leans her cheek upon her hand! Oh, that I were a glove upon that hand, that I might touch that cheek!

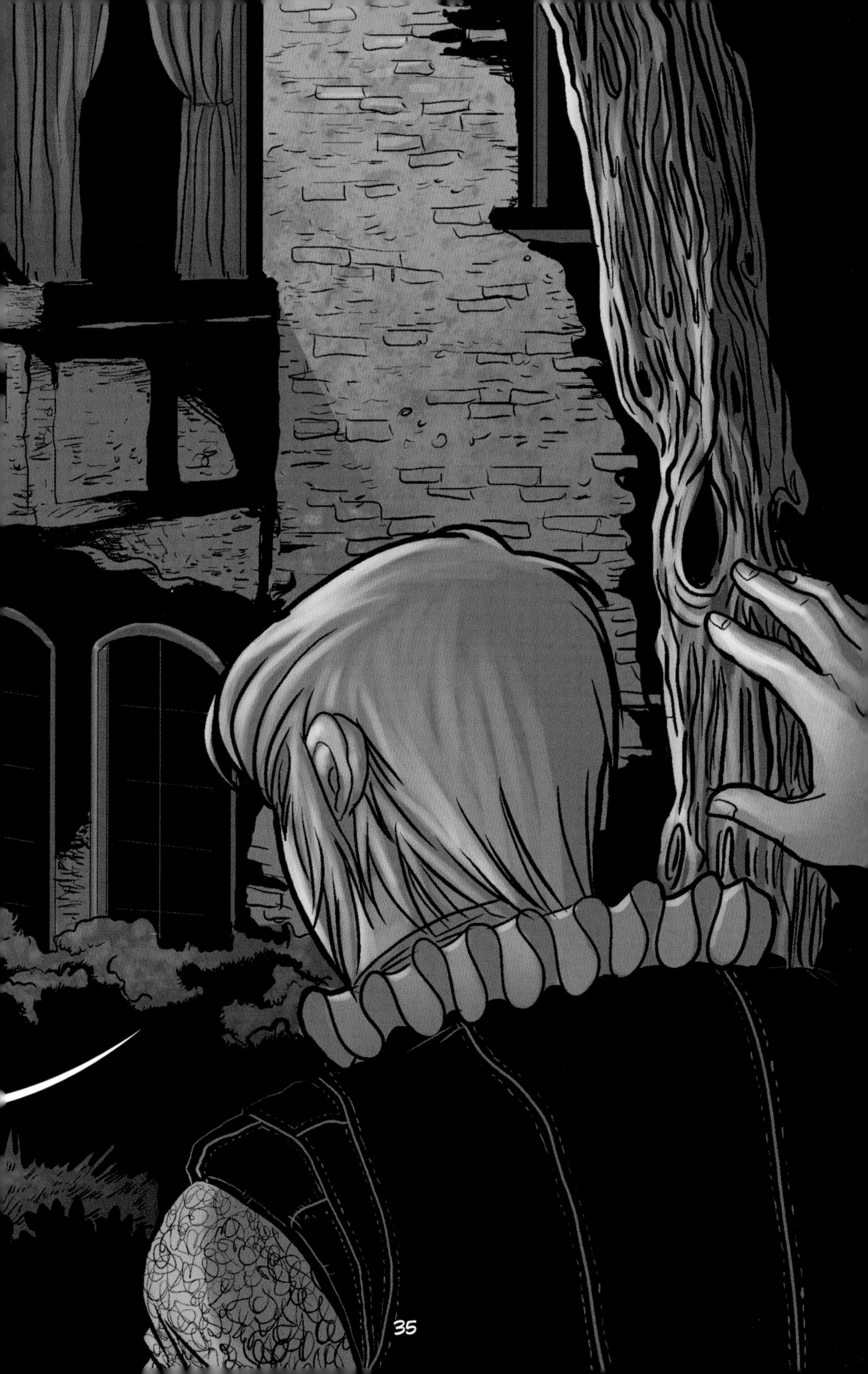

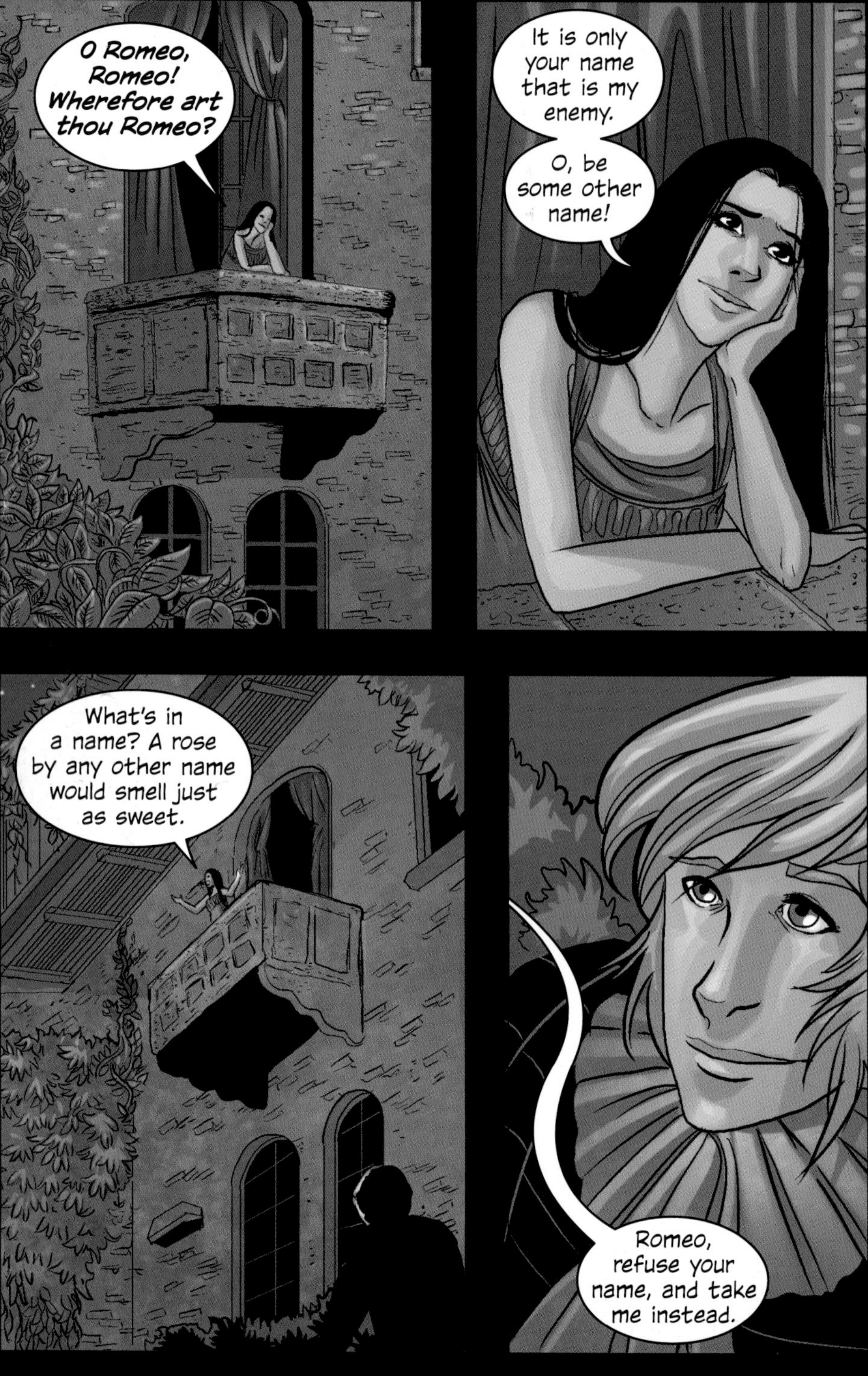
O Romeo, Romeo! Wherefore art thou Romeo?
It is only your name that is my enemy.
O, be some other name!
What's in a name? A rose by any other name would smell just as sweet.
Romeo, refuse your name, and take me instead.

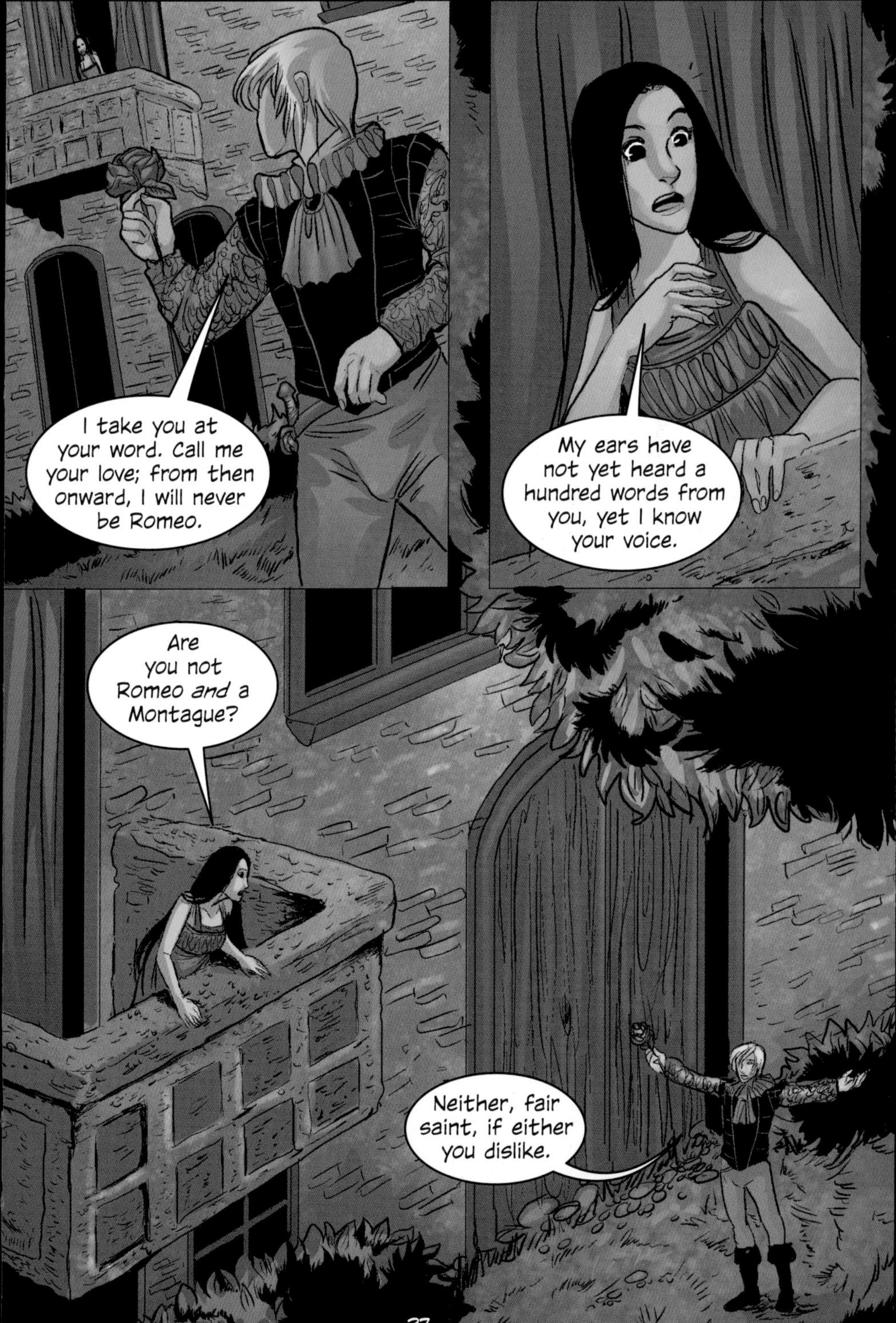
I take you at your word. Call me your love; from then onward, I will never be Romeo.
My ears have not yet heard a hundred words from you, yet I know your voice.
Are you not Romeo *and* a Montague?
Neither, fair saint, if either you dislike.

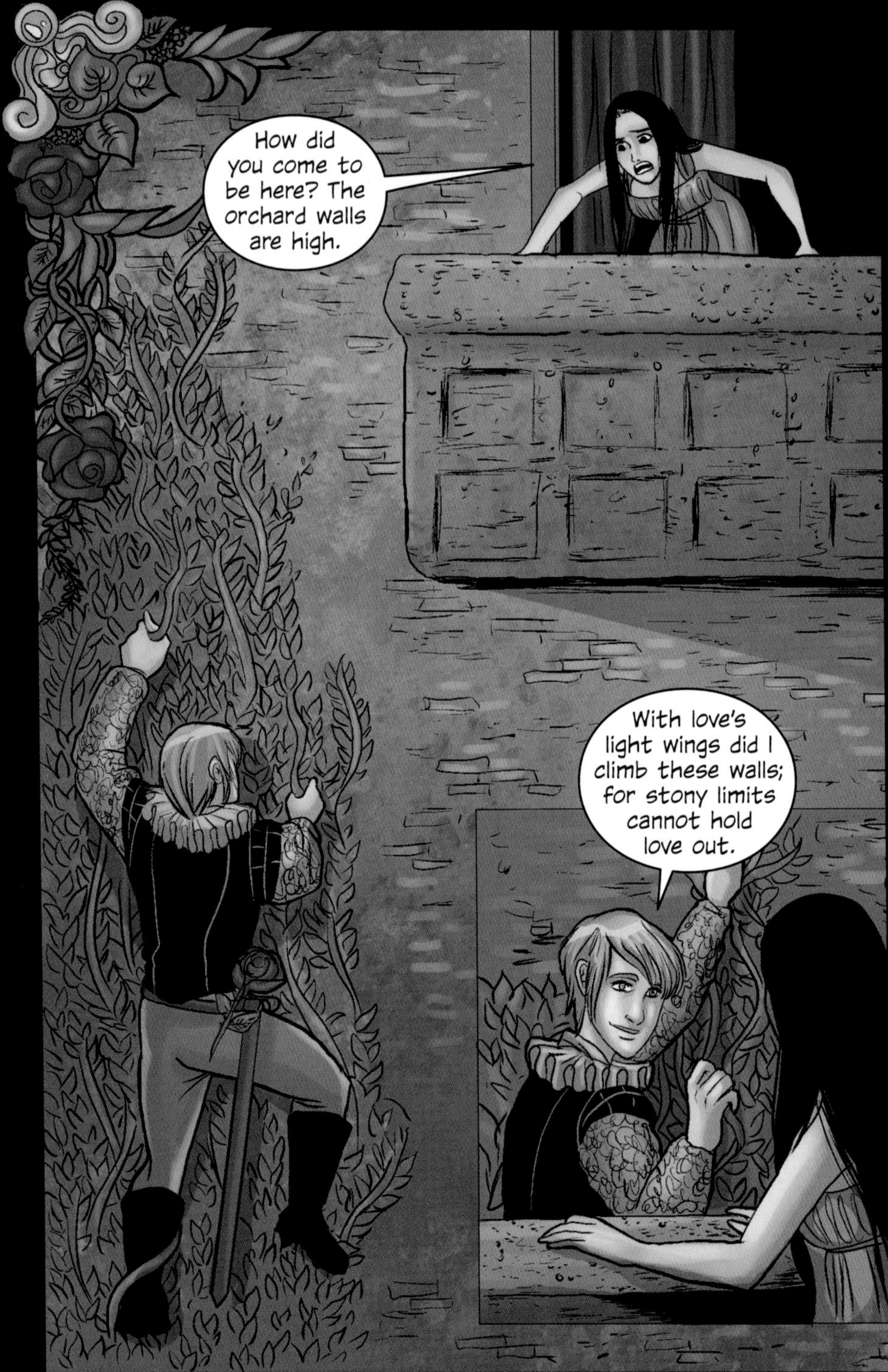
How did you come to be here? The orchard walls are high.
With love's light wings did I climb these walls; for stony limits cannot hold love out.

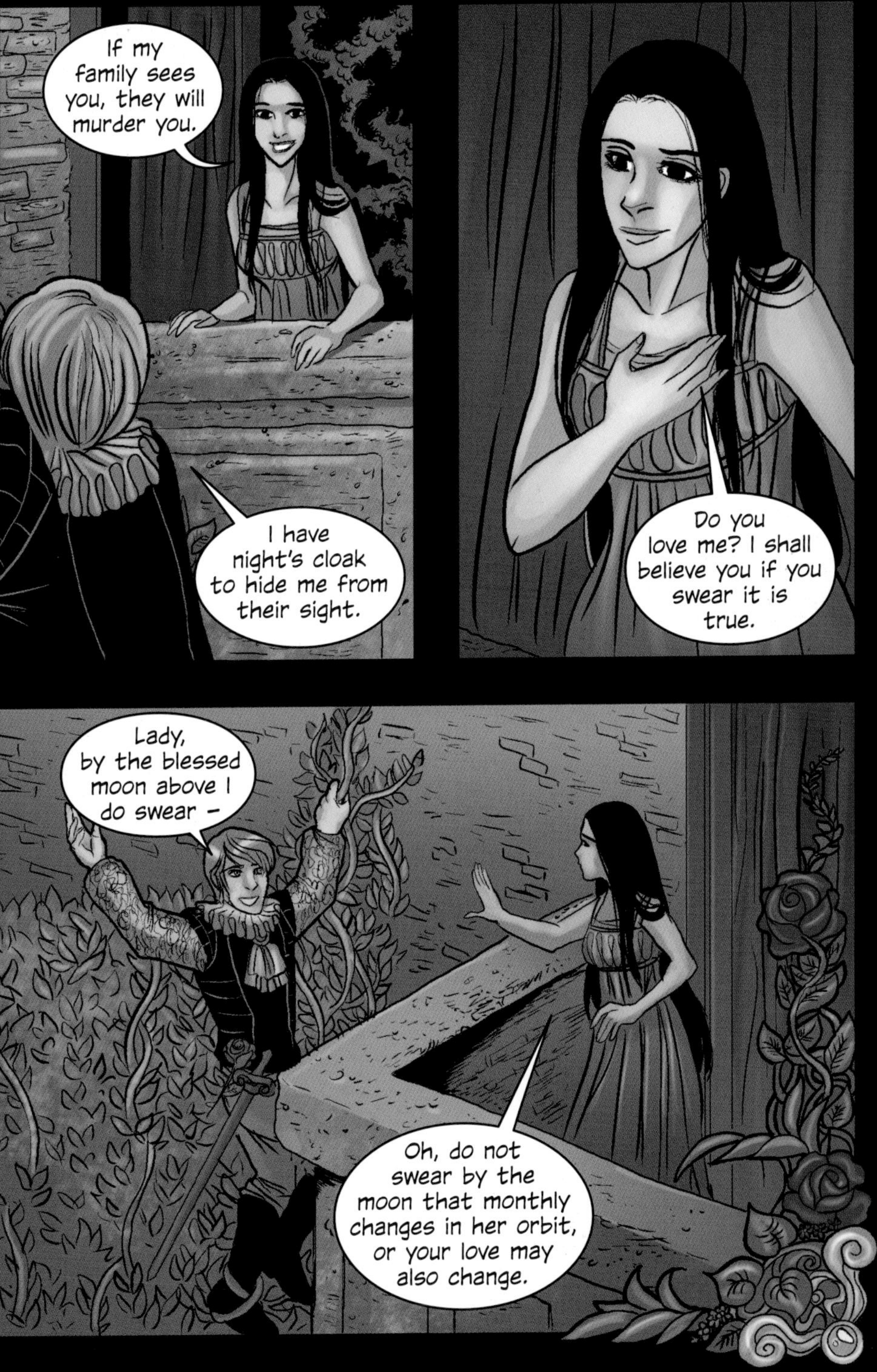
If my family sees you, they will murder you.
I have night's cloak to hide me from their sight.
Do you love me? I shall believe you if you swear it is true.
Lady, by the blessed moon above I do swear –
Oh, do not swear by the moon that monthly changes in her orbit, or your love may also change.

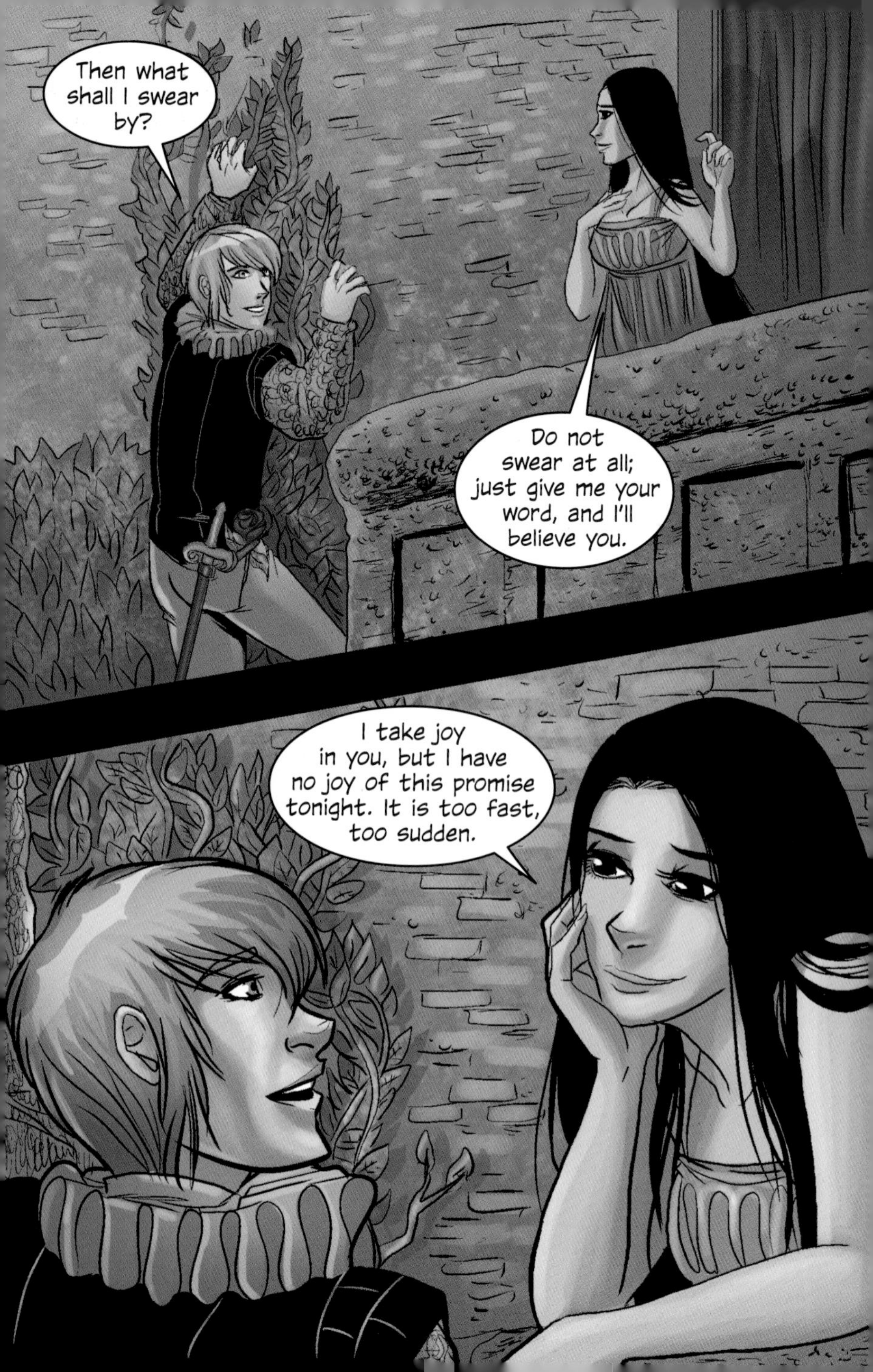
Then what shall I swear by?
Do not swear at all; just give me your word, and I'll believe you.
I take joy in you, but I have no joy of this promise tonight. It is too fast, too sudden.

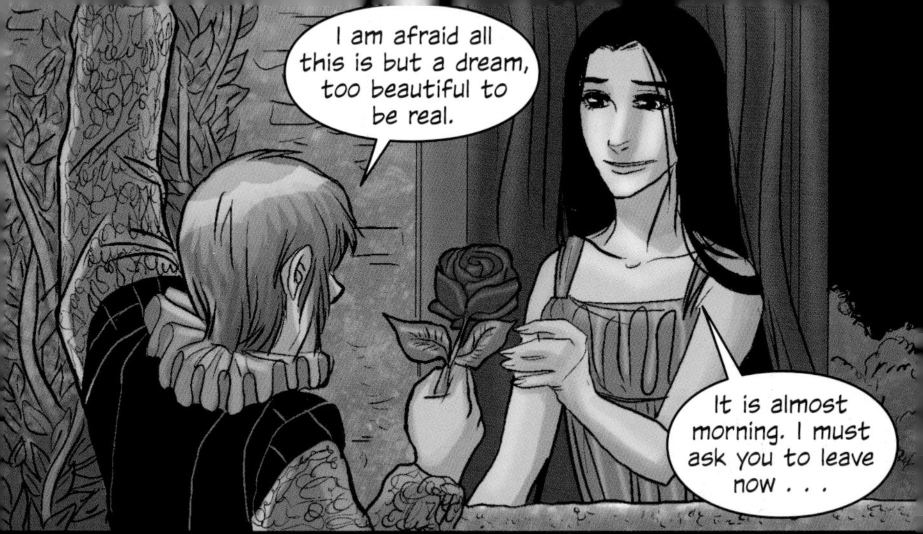
I am afraid all this is but a dream, too beautiful to be real.
It is almost morning. I must ask you to leave now . . .

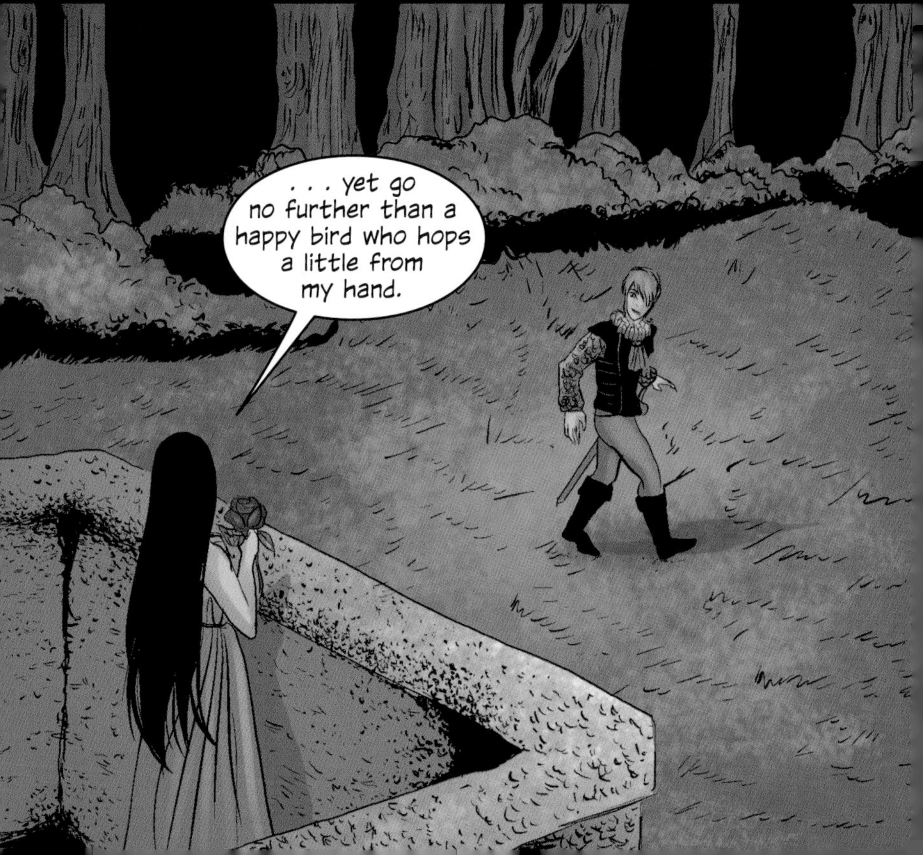
. . . yet go no further than a happy bird who hops a little from my hand.

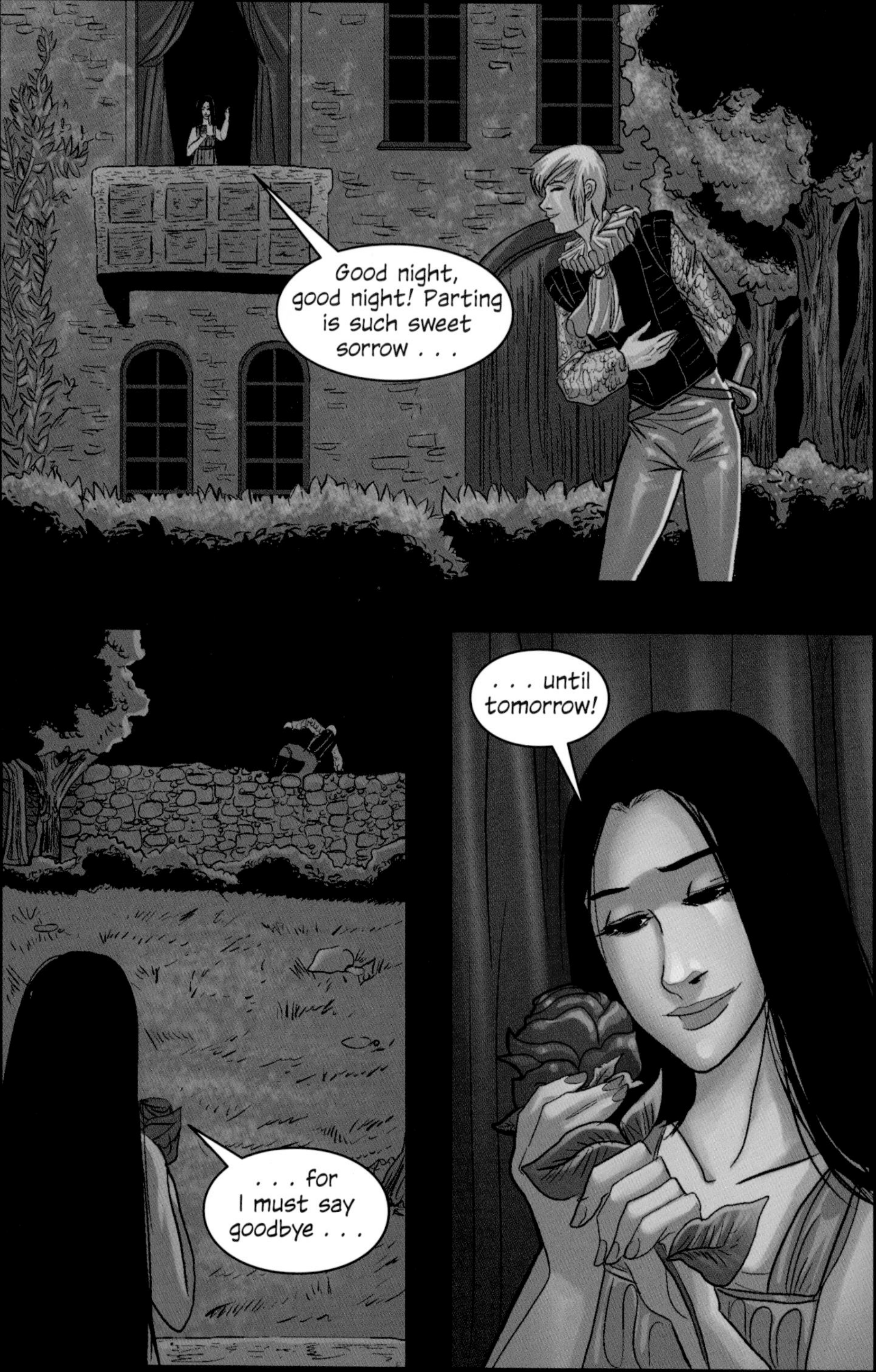
Good night, good night! Parting is such sweet sorrow . . .
. . . for I must say goodbye . . .
. . . until tomorrow!

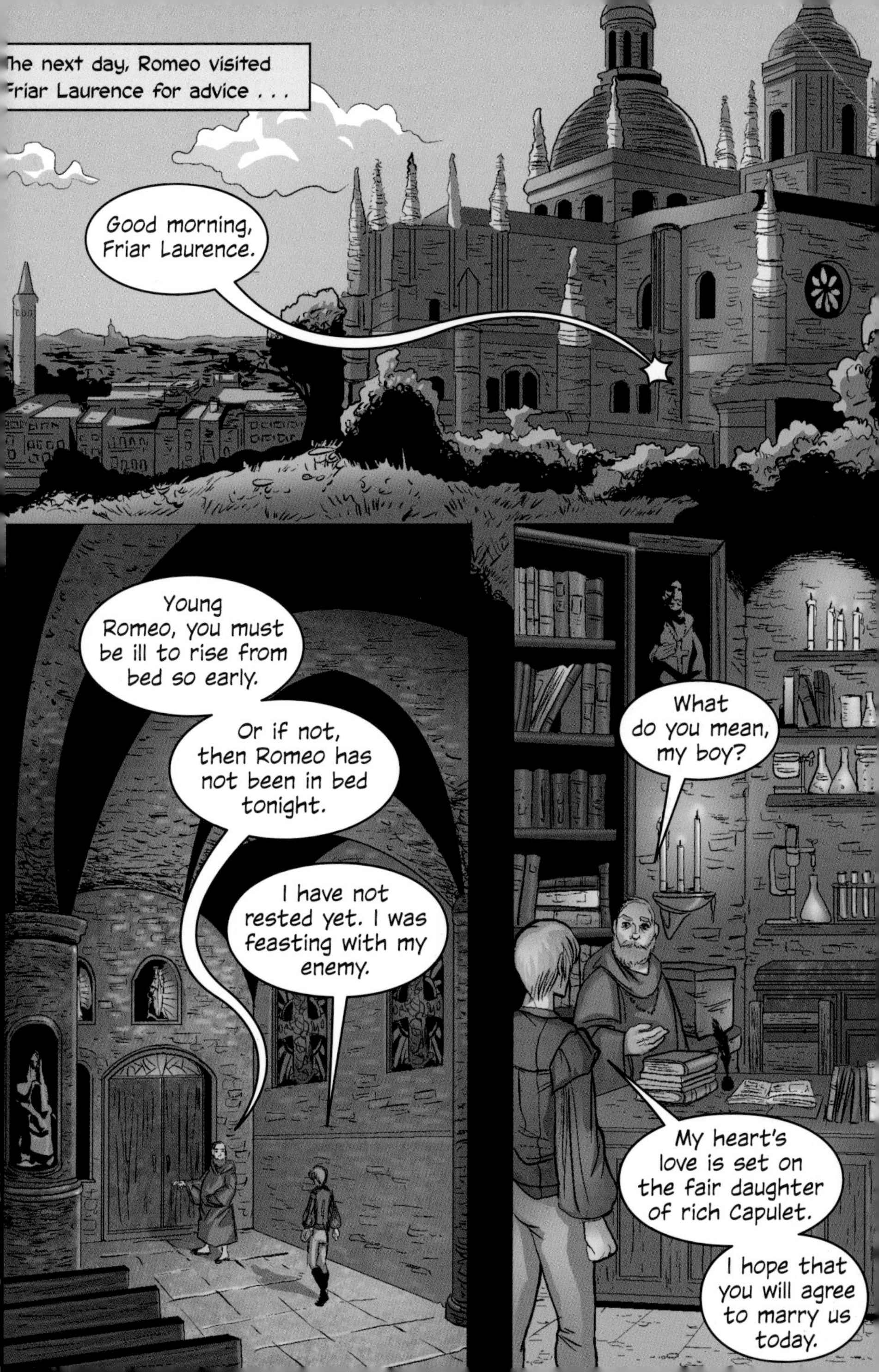
The next day, Romeo visited Friar Laurence for advice . . .
Good morning, Friar Laurence.
Young Romeo, you must be ill to rise from bed so early.
Or if not, then Romeo has not been in bed tonight.
I have not rested yet. I was feasting with my enemy.
What do you mean, my boy?
My heart's love is set on the fair daughter of rich Capulet.
I hope that you will agree to marry us today.

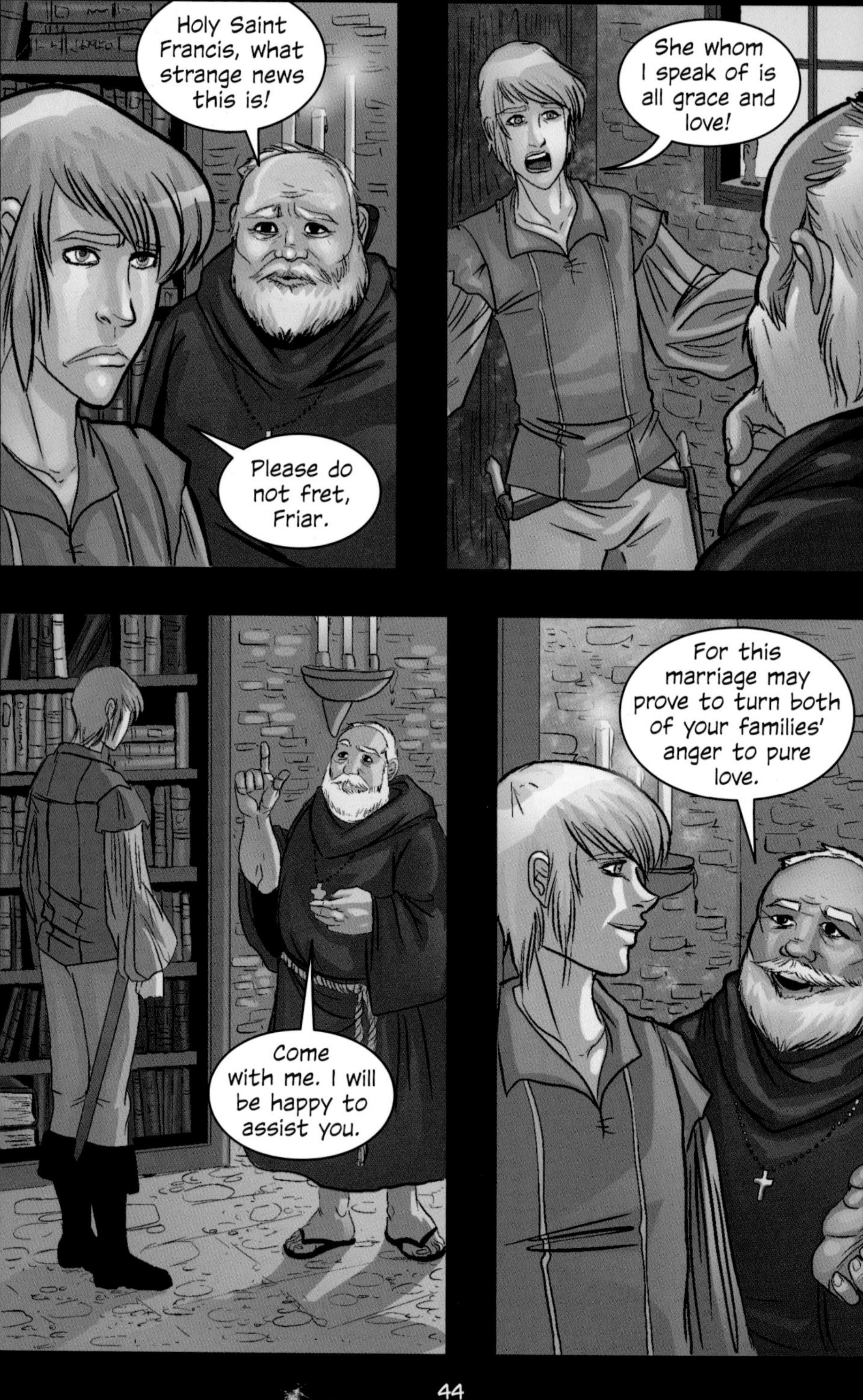
Holy Saint Francis, what strange news this is!
Please do not fret, Friar.
She whom I speak of is all grace and love!
Come with me. I will be happy to assist you.
For this marriage may prove to turn both of your families' anger to pure love.

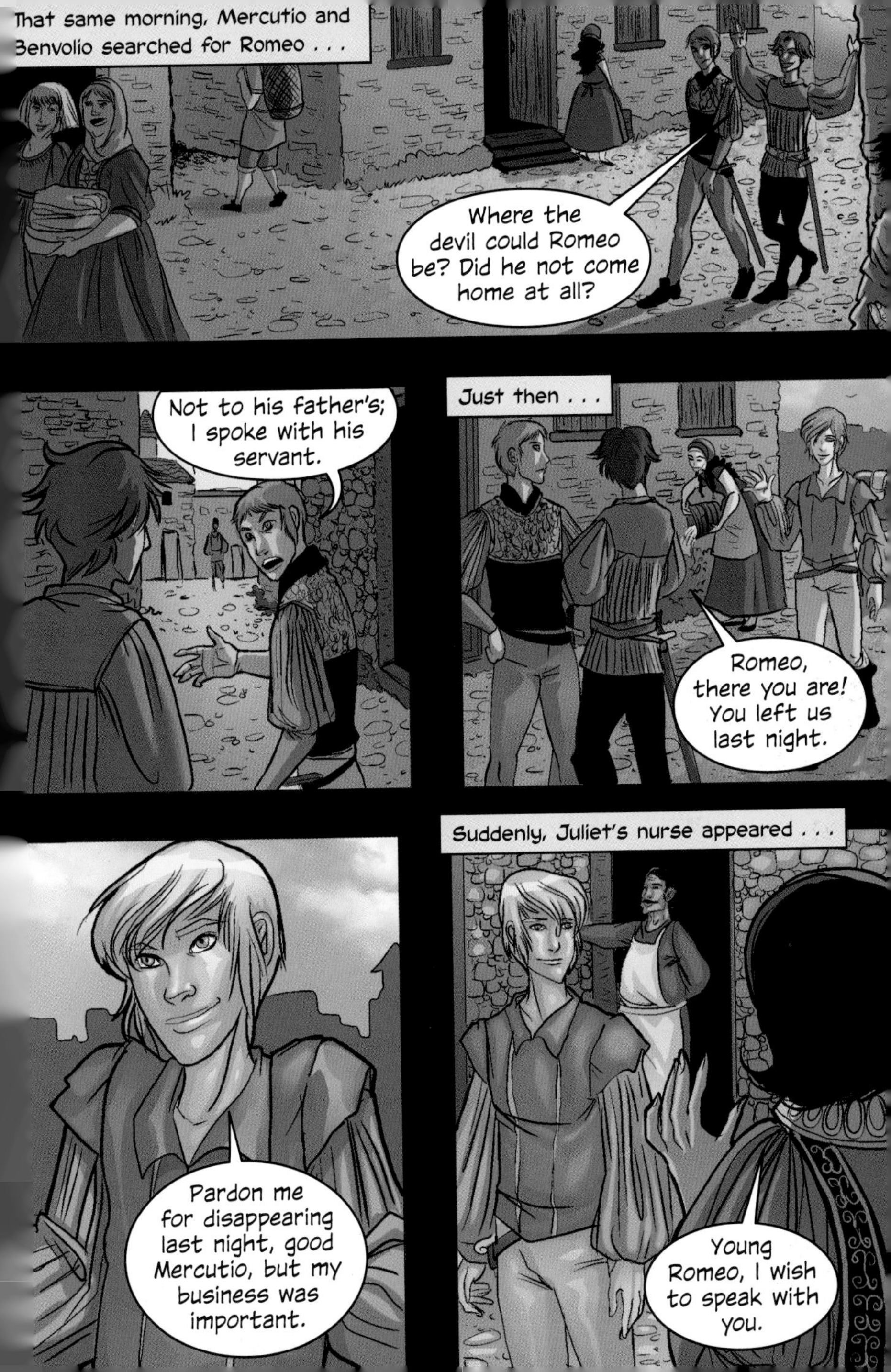
That same morning, Mercutio and Benvolio searched for Romeo . . .
Where the devil could Romeo be? Did he not come home at all?
Not to his father's; I spoke with his servant.
Just then . . .
Romeo, there you are! You left us last night.
Pardon me for disappearing last night, good Mercutio, but my business was important.
Suddenly, Juliet's nurse appeared . . .
Young Romeo, I wish to speak with you.

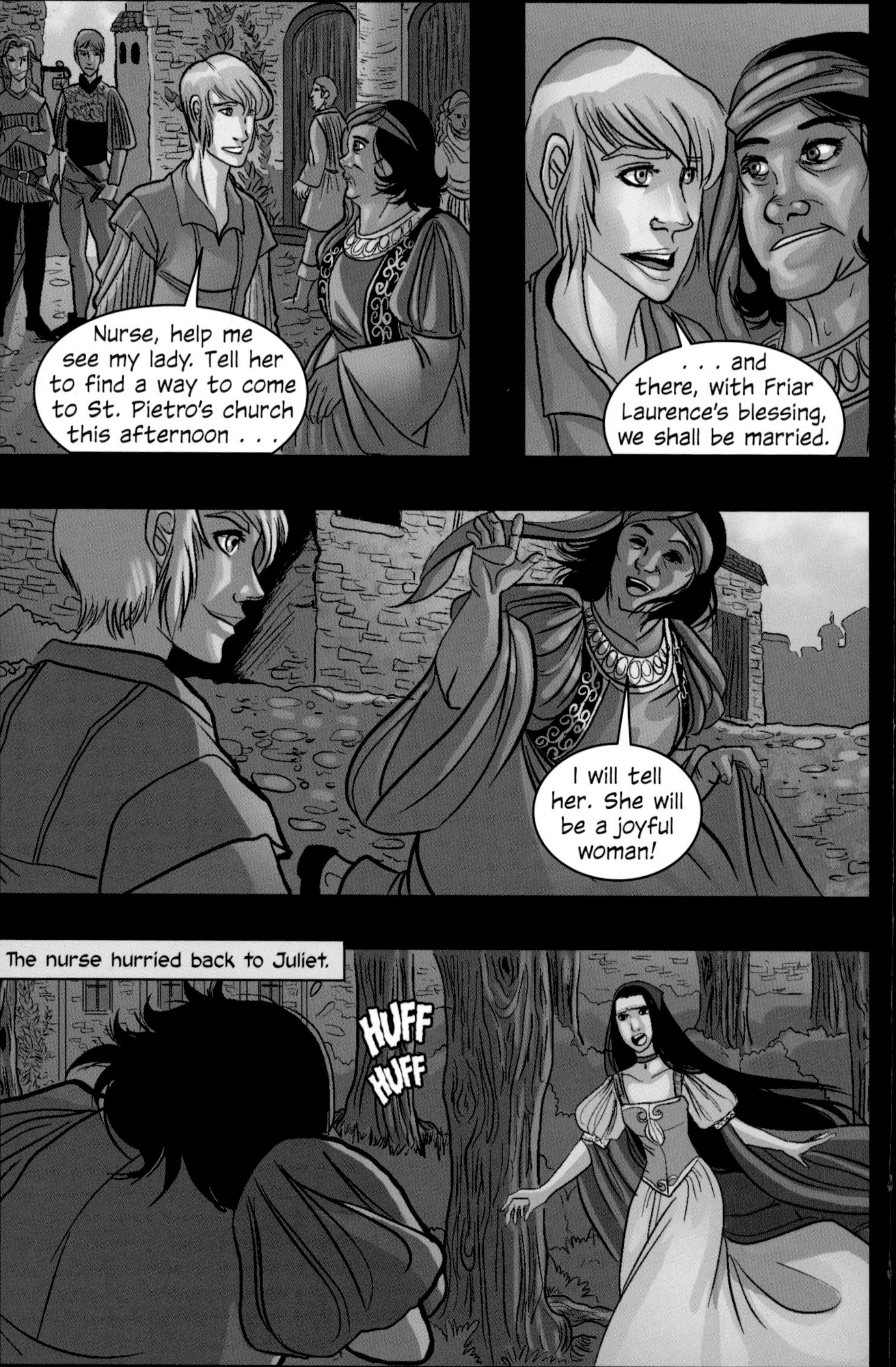
Nurse, help me see my lady. Tell her to find a way to come to St. Pietro's church this afternoon . . .
. . . and there, with Friar Laurence's blessing, we shall be married.
I will tell her. She will be a joyful woman!
The nurse hurried back to Juliet.
HUFF HUFF

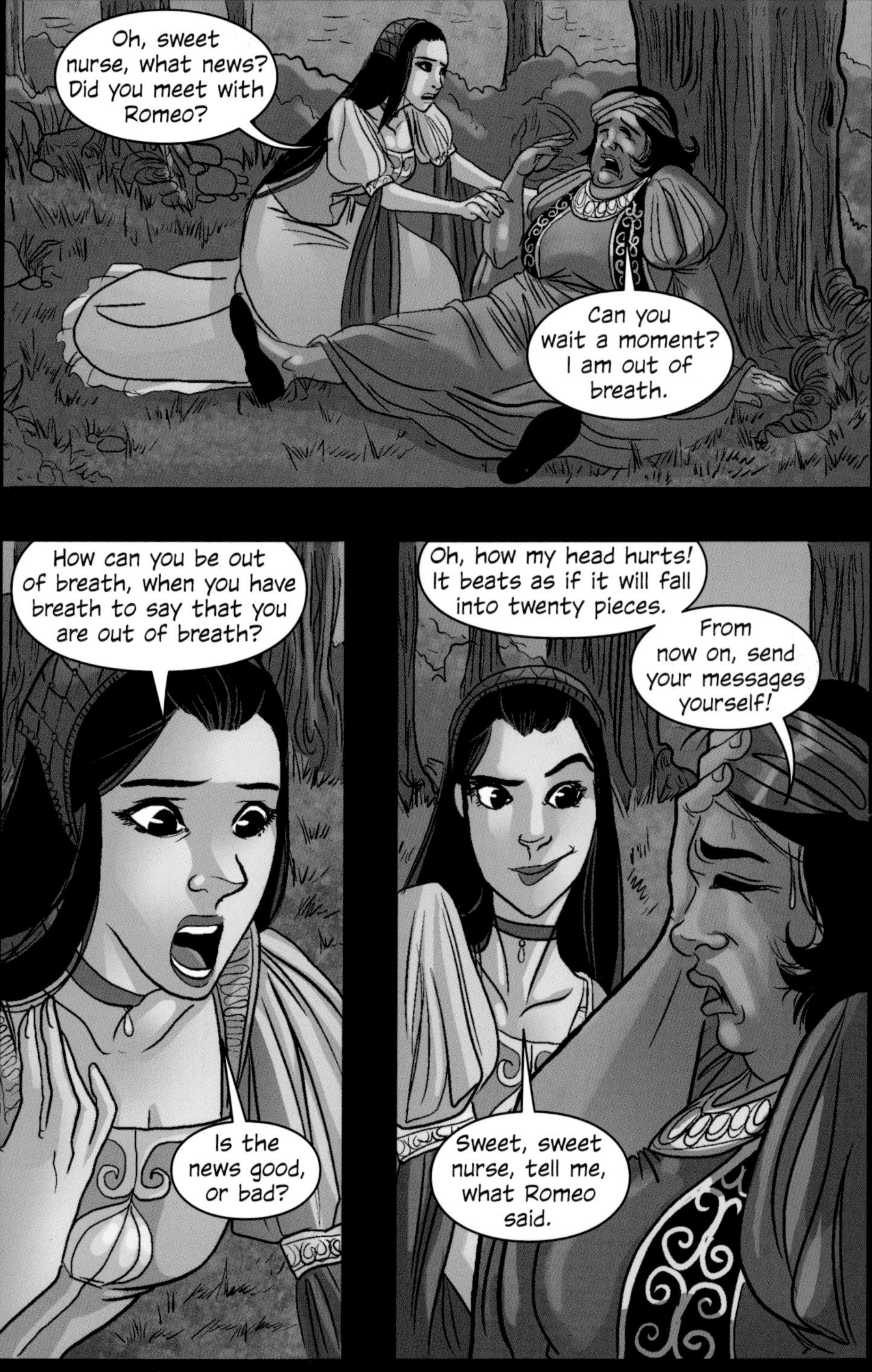
Oh, sweet nurse, what news? Did you meet with Romeo?
Can you wait a moment? I am out of breath.
How can you be out of breath, when you have breath to say that you are out of breath?
Is the news good, or bad?
Oh, how my head hurts! It beats as if it will fall into twenty pieces.
From now on, send your messages yourself!
Sweet, sweet nurse, tell me, what Romeo said.

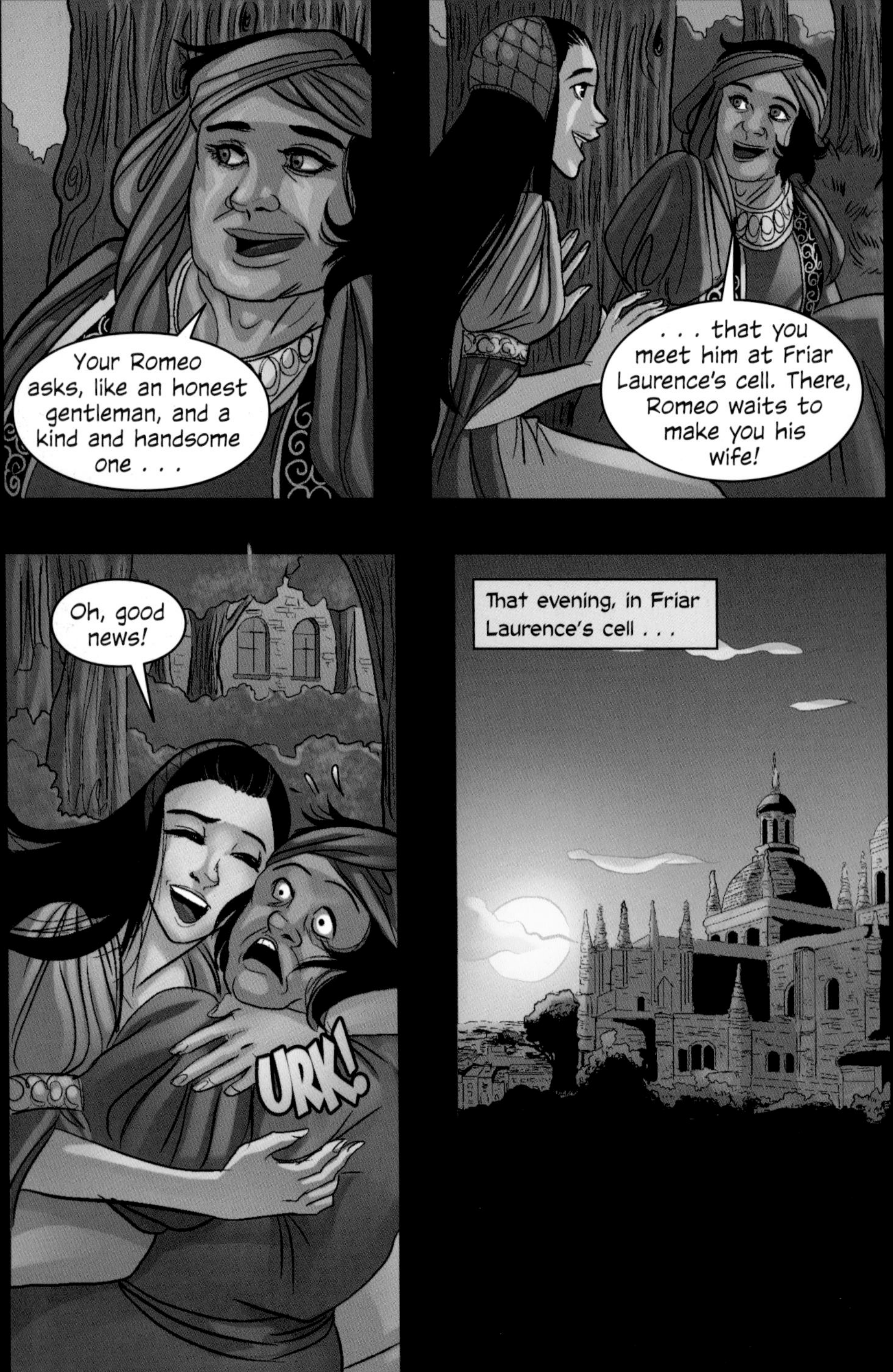
Your Romeo asks, like an honest gentleman, and a kind and handsome one . . .
. . . that you meet him at Friar Laurence's cell. There, Romeo waits to make you his wife!
Oh, good news!
URK!
That evening, in Friar Laurence's cell . . .

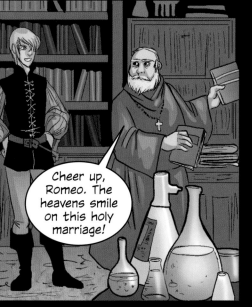

Cheer up, Romeo. The heavens smile on this holy marriage!

You will unite our lives with holy words, until death do part us.

Here comes the lady!

Then I may call her mine.

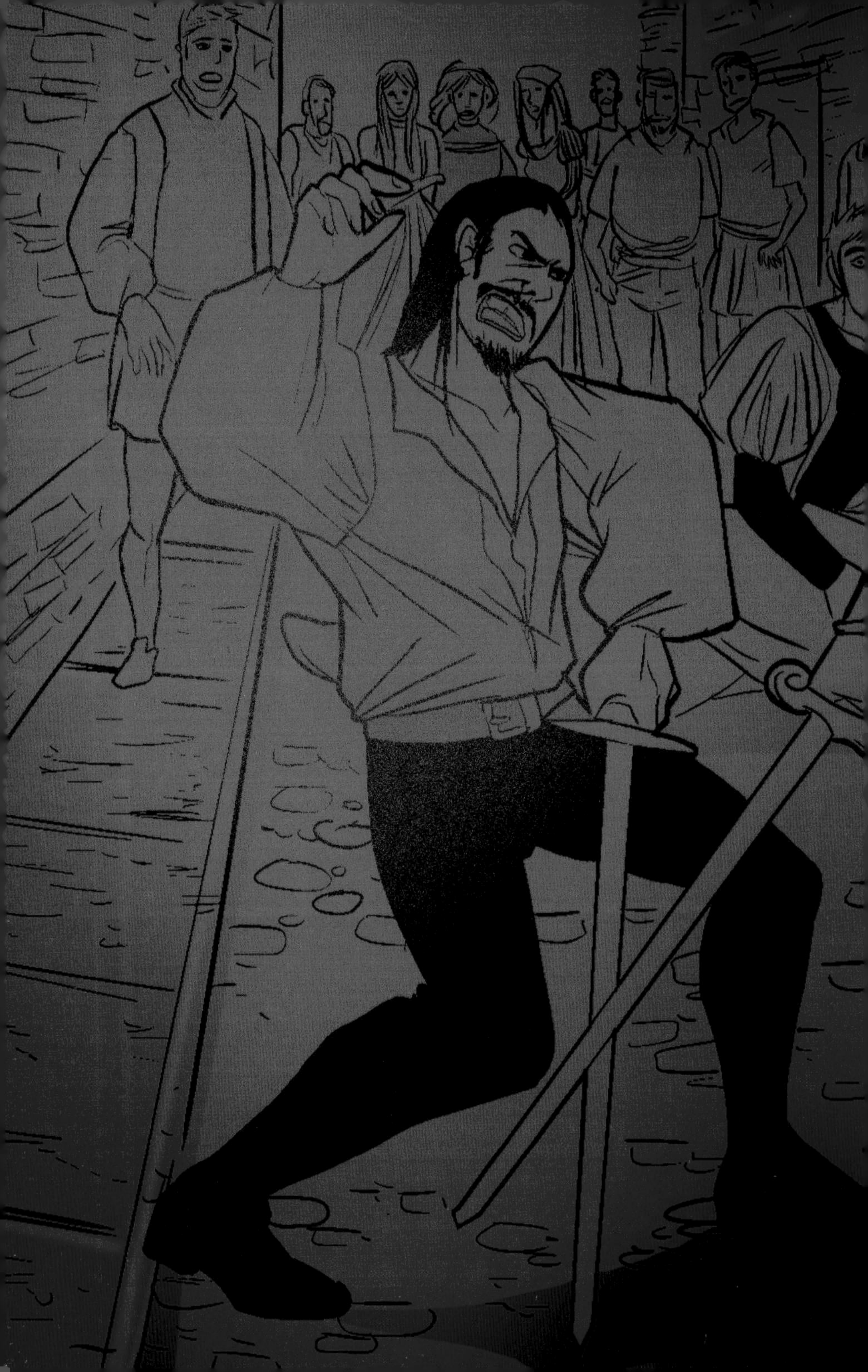

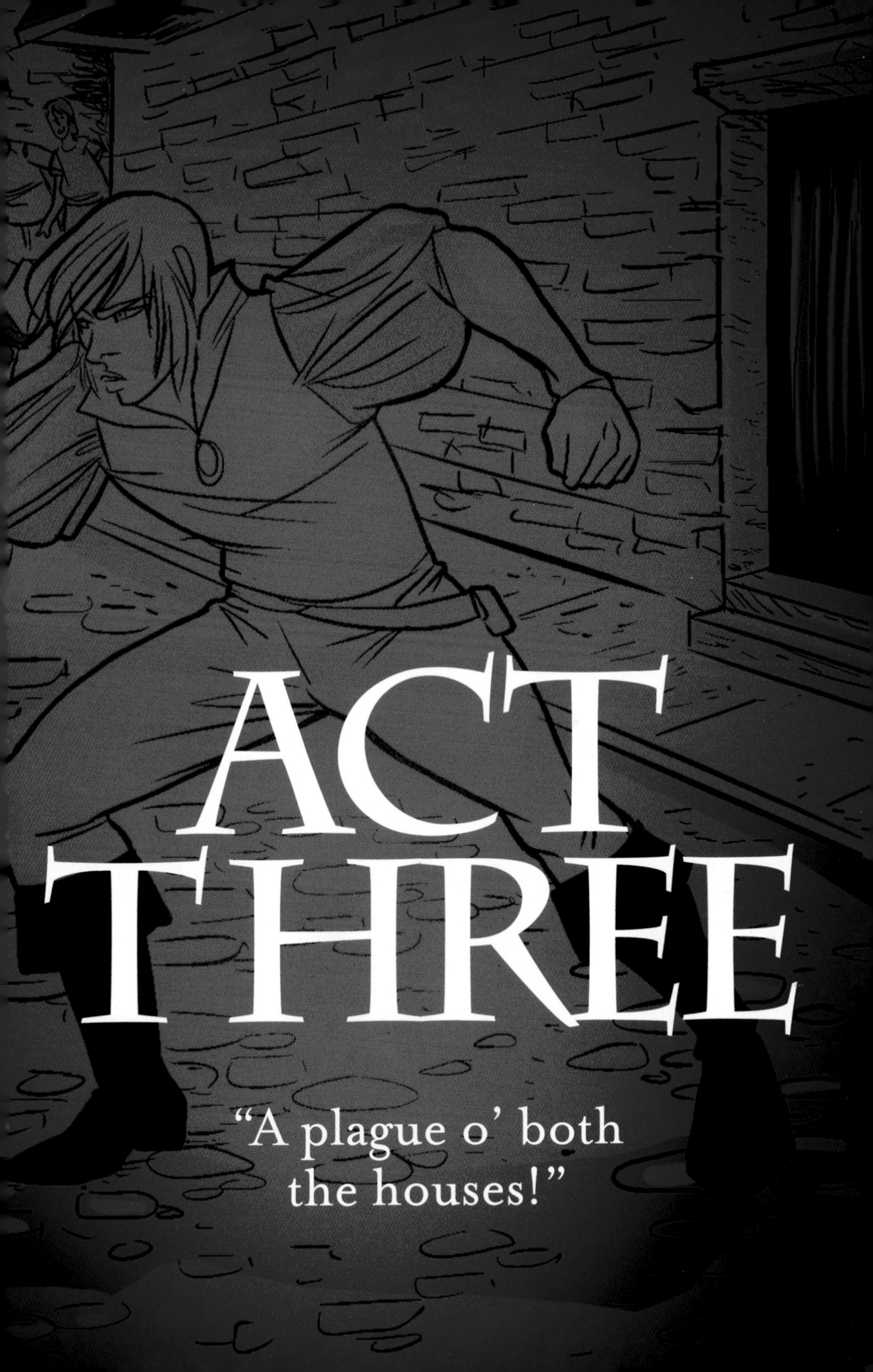

ACT THREE

"A plague o' both the houses!"

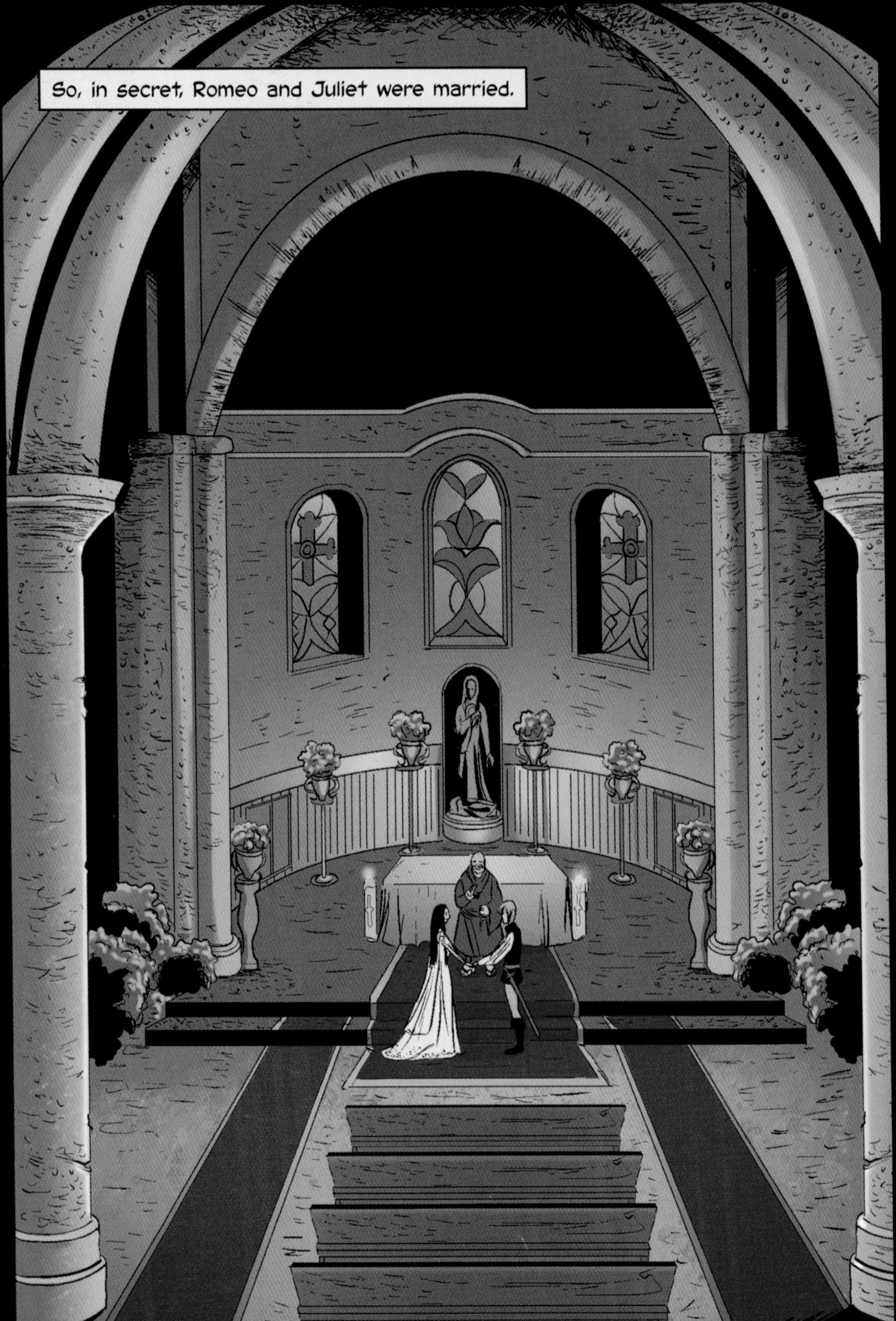
So, in secret, Romeo and Juliet were married.

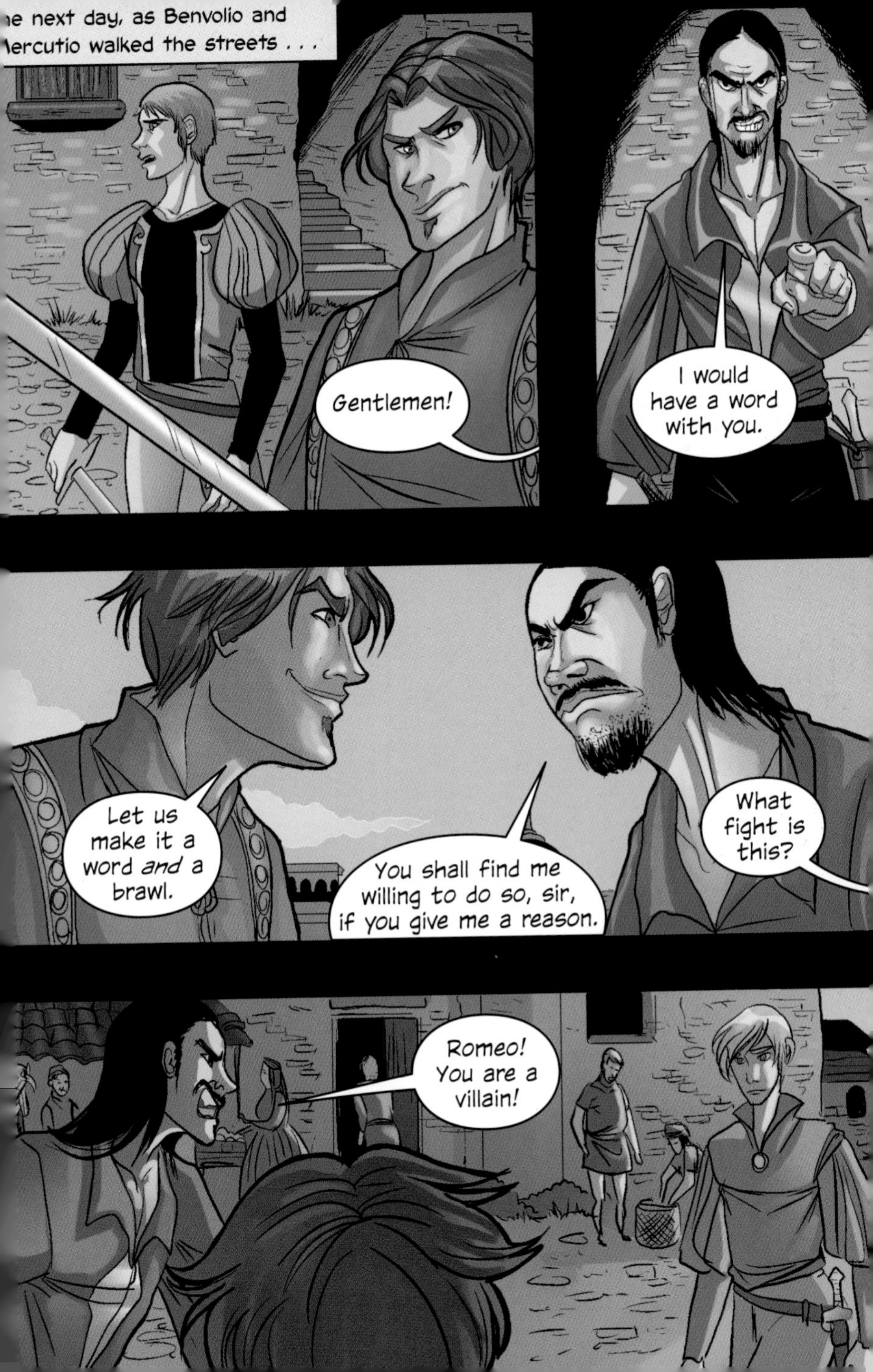

ne next day, as Benvolio and
Mercutio walked the streets . . .
Gentlemen!
I would have a word with you.
Let us make it a word *and* a brawl.
You shall find me willing to do so, sir, if you give me a reason.
What fight is this?
Romeo! You are a villain!

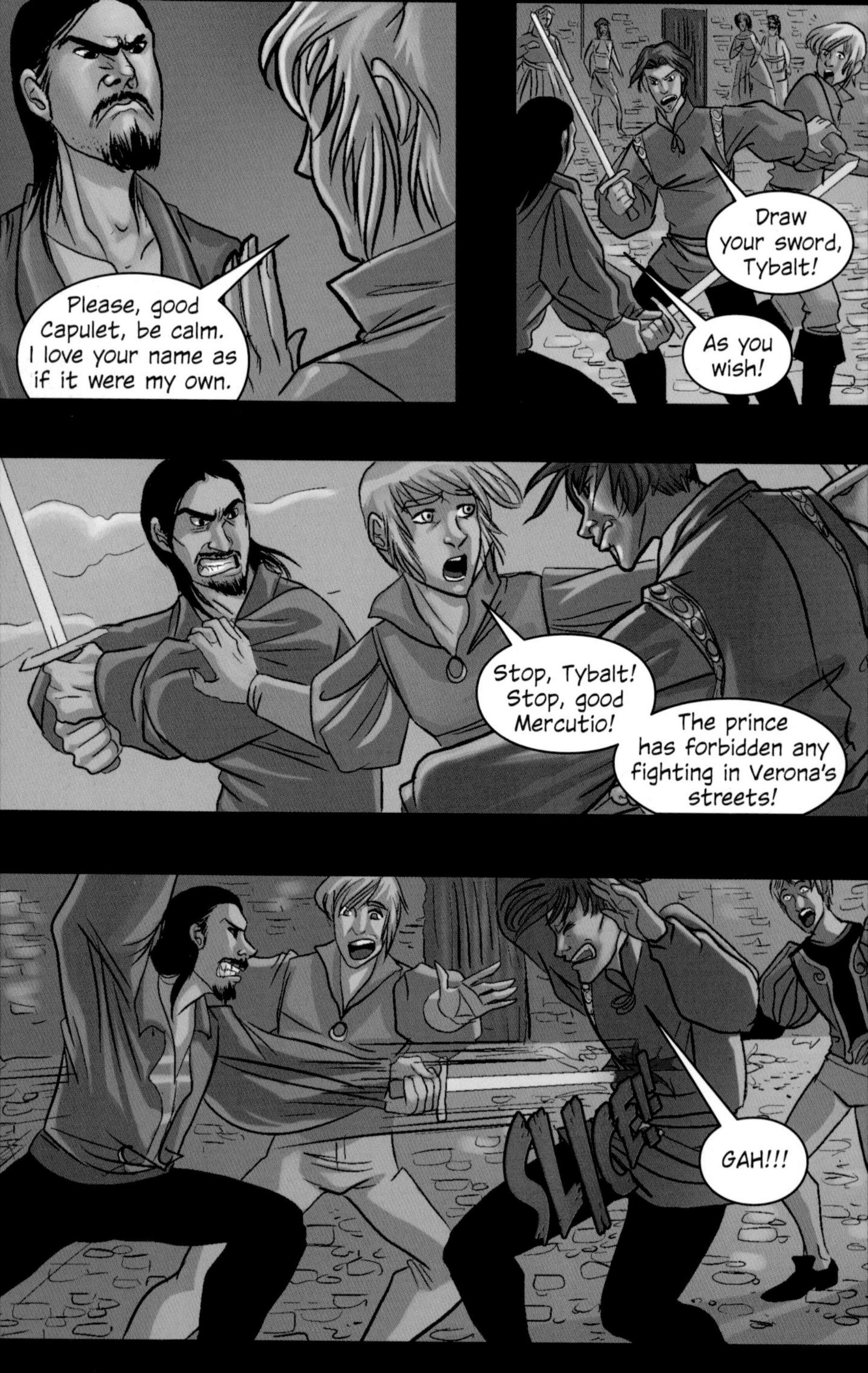
Please, good Capulet, be calm. I love your name as if it were my own.
Draw your sword, Tybalt!
As you wish!
Stop, Tybalt! Stop, good Mercutio!
The prince has forbidden any fighting in Verona's streets!
SLICE!
GAH!!!

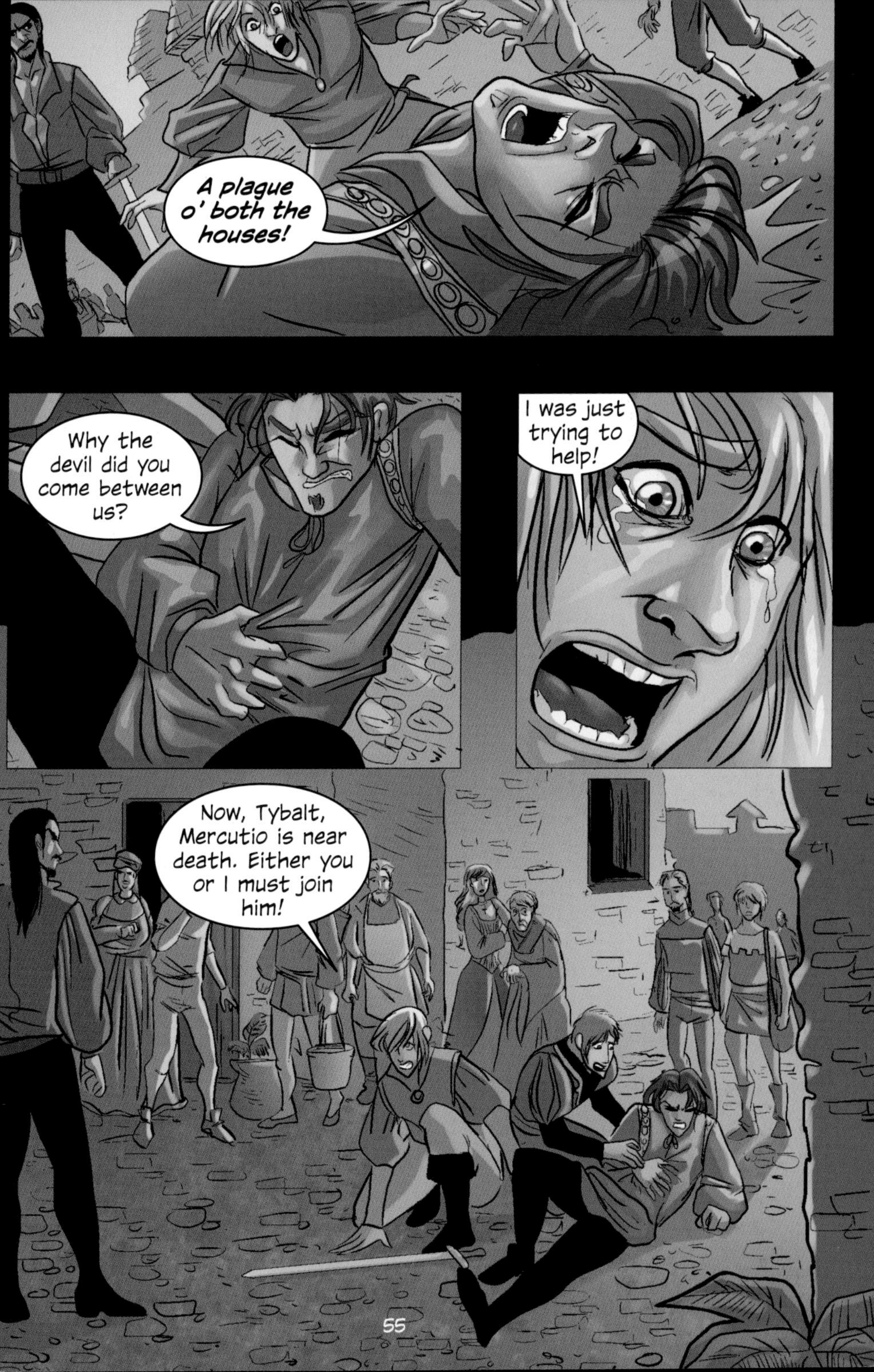
A plague o' both the houses!
Why the devil did you come between us?
I was just trying to help!
Now, Tybalt, Mercutio is near death. Either you or I must join him!

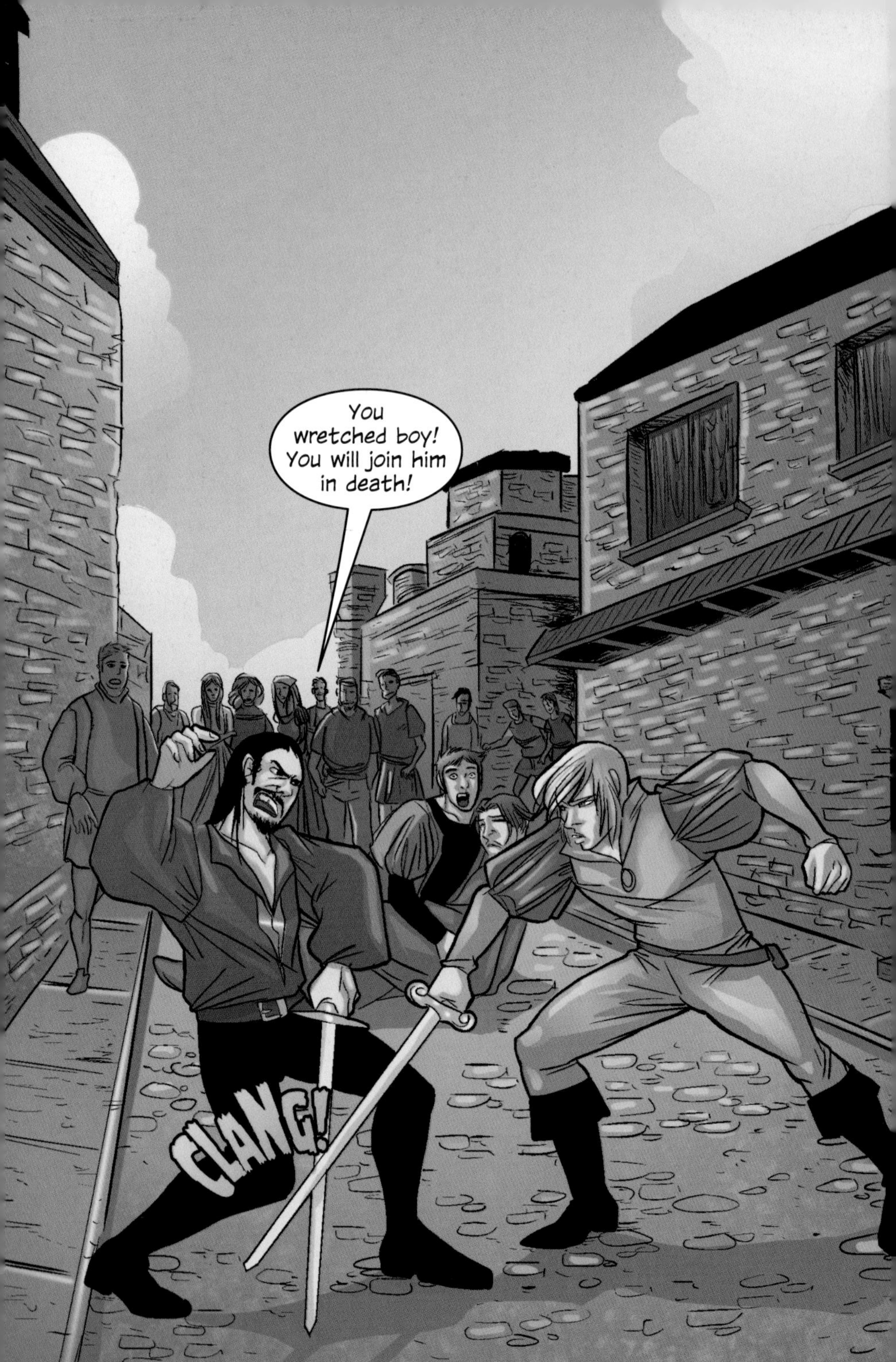
You wretched boy! You will join him in death!
CLANG!

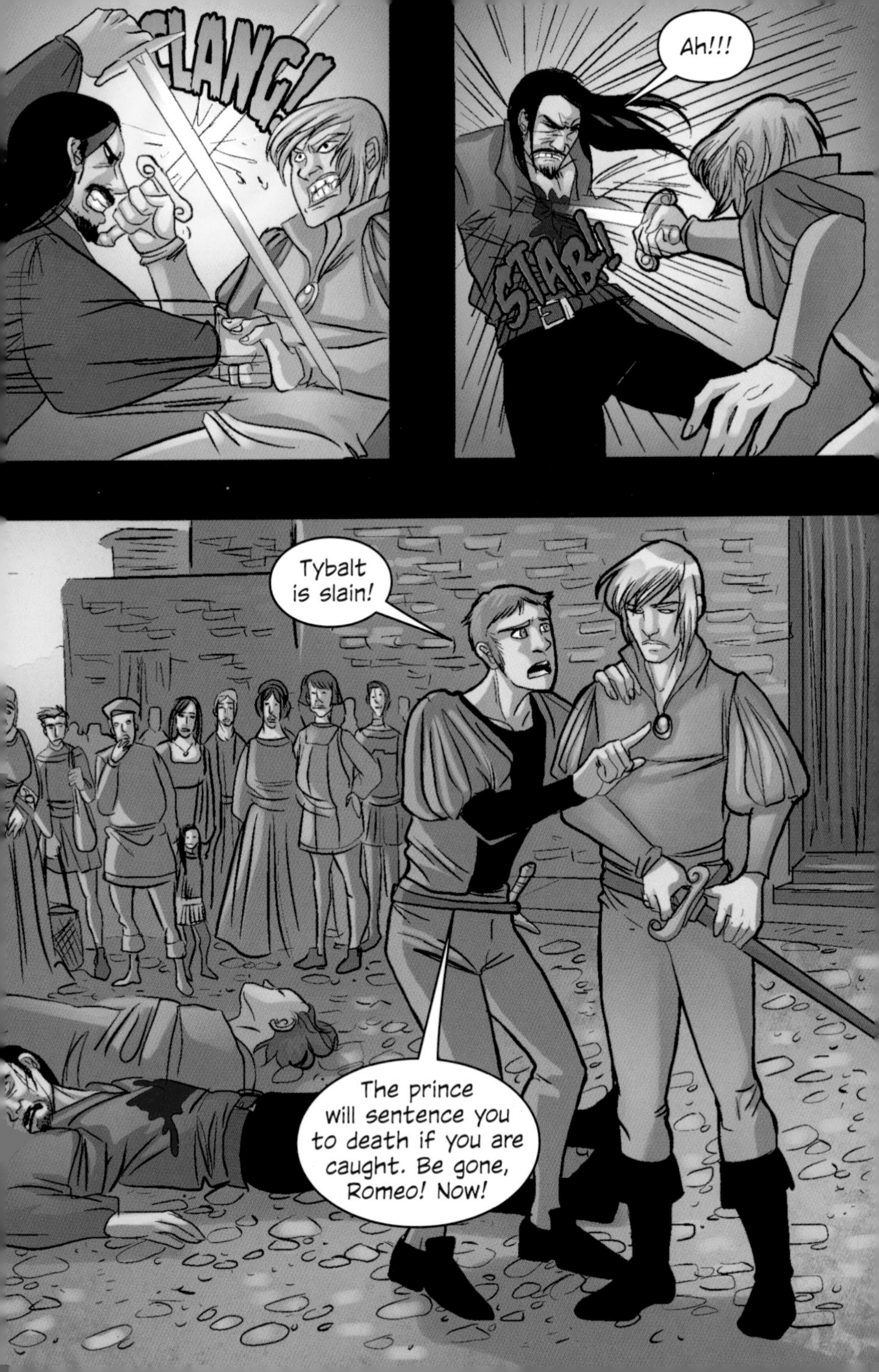
CLANG!
Ah!!!
STAB!
Tybalt is slain!
The prince will sentence you to death if you are caught. Be gone, Romeo! Now!

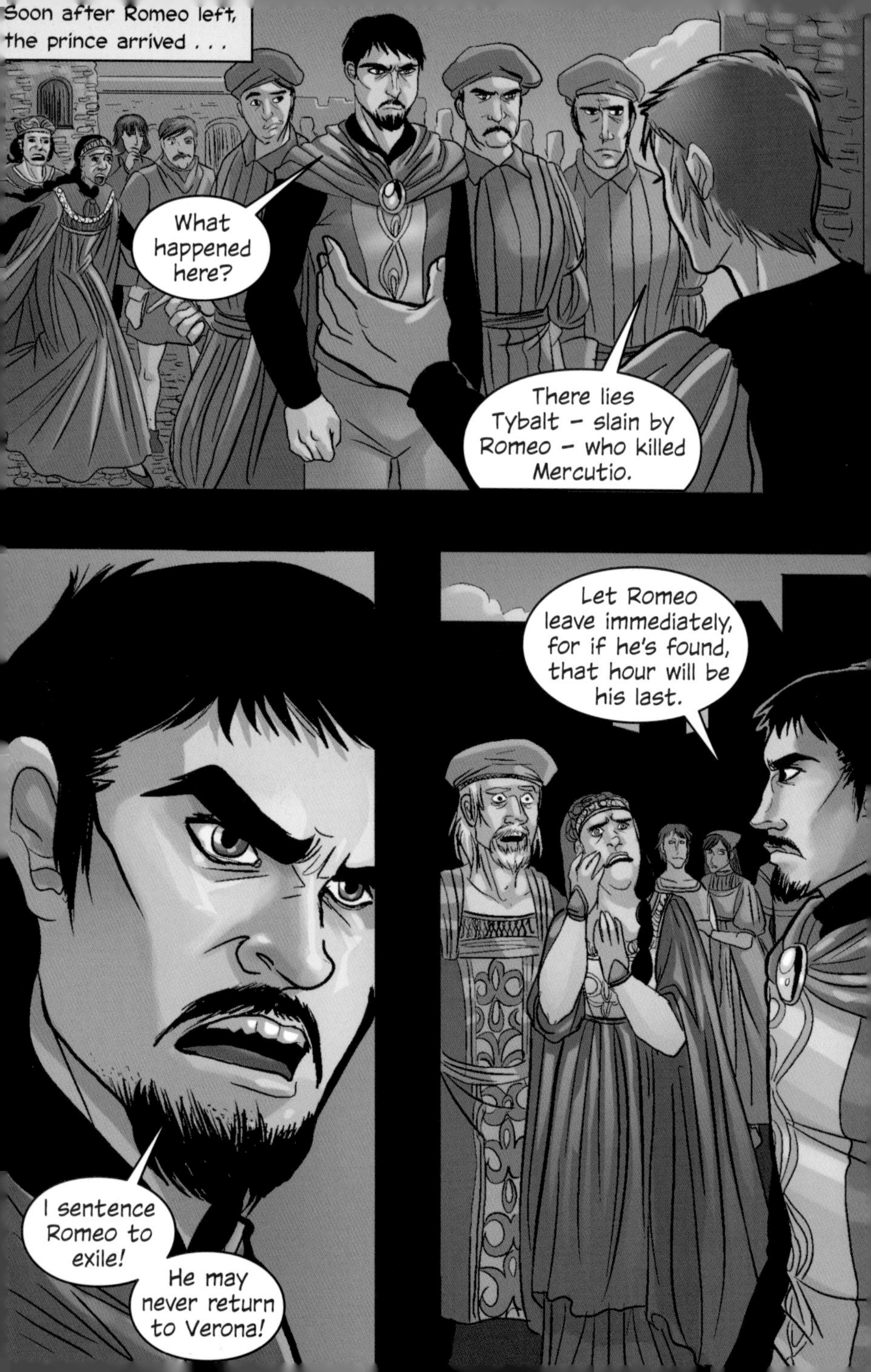
Soon after Romeo left, the prince arrived . . .
What happened here?
There lies Tybalt – slain by Romeo – who killed Mercutio.
I sentence Romeo to exile!
He may never return to Verona!
Let Romeo leave immediately, for if he's found, that hour will be his last.

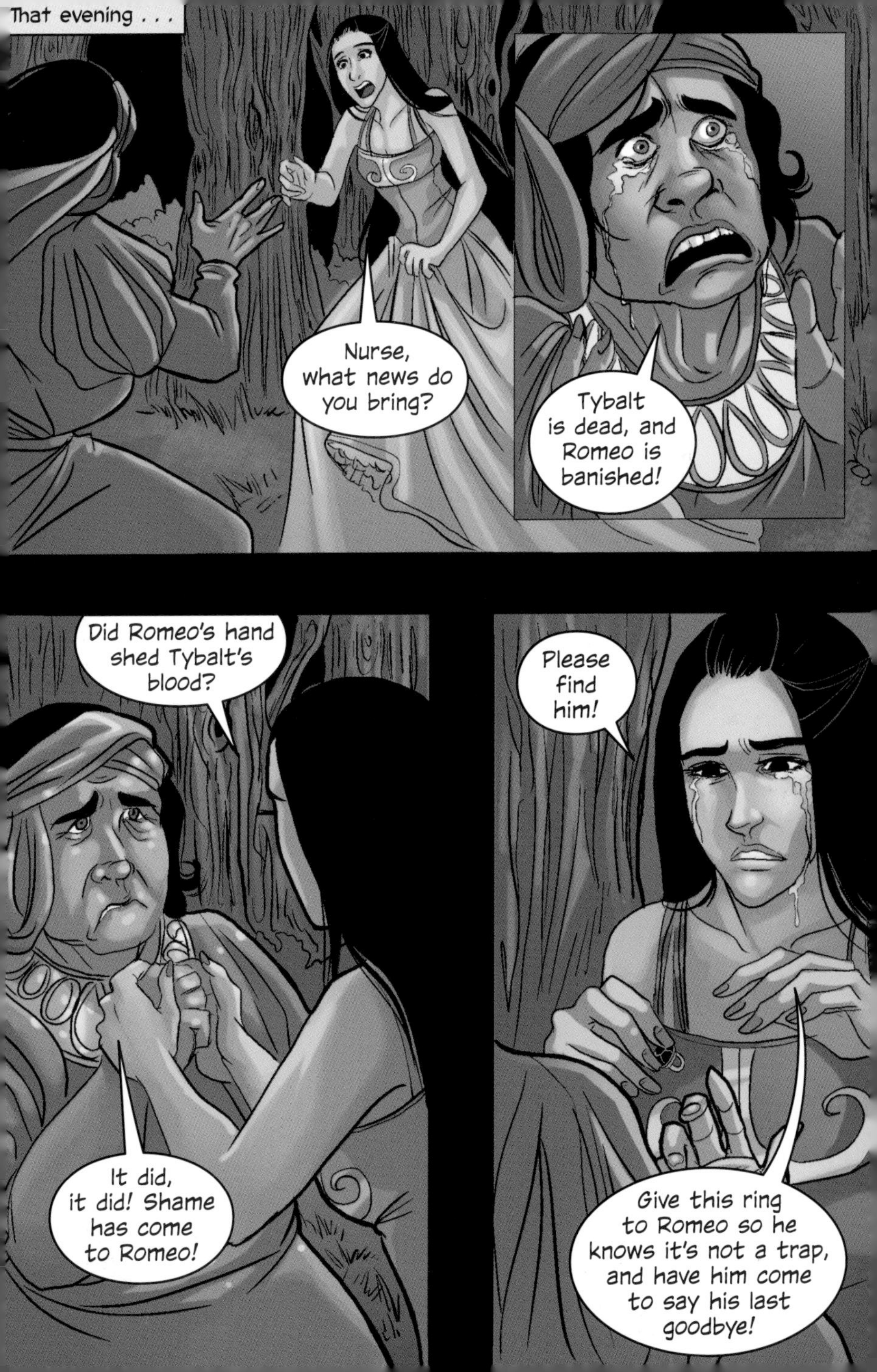
That evening . . .
Nurse, what news do you bring?
Tybalt is dead, and Romeo is banished!
Did Romeo's hand shed Tybalt's blood?
It did, it did! Shame has come to Romeo!
Please find him!
Give this ring to Romeo so he knows it's not a trap, and have him come to say his last goodbye!

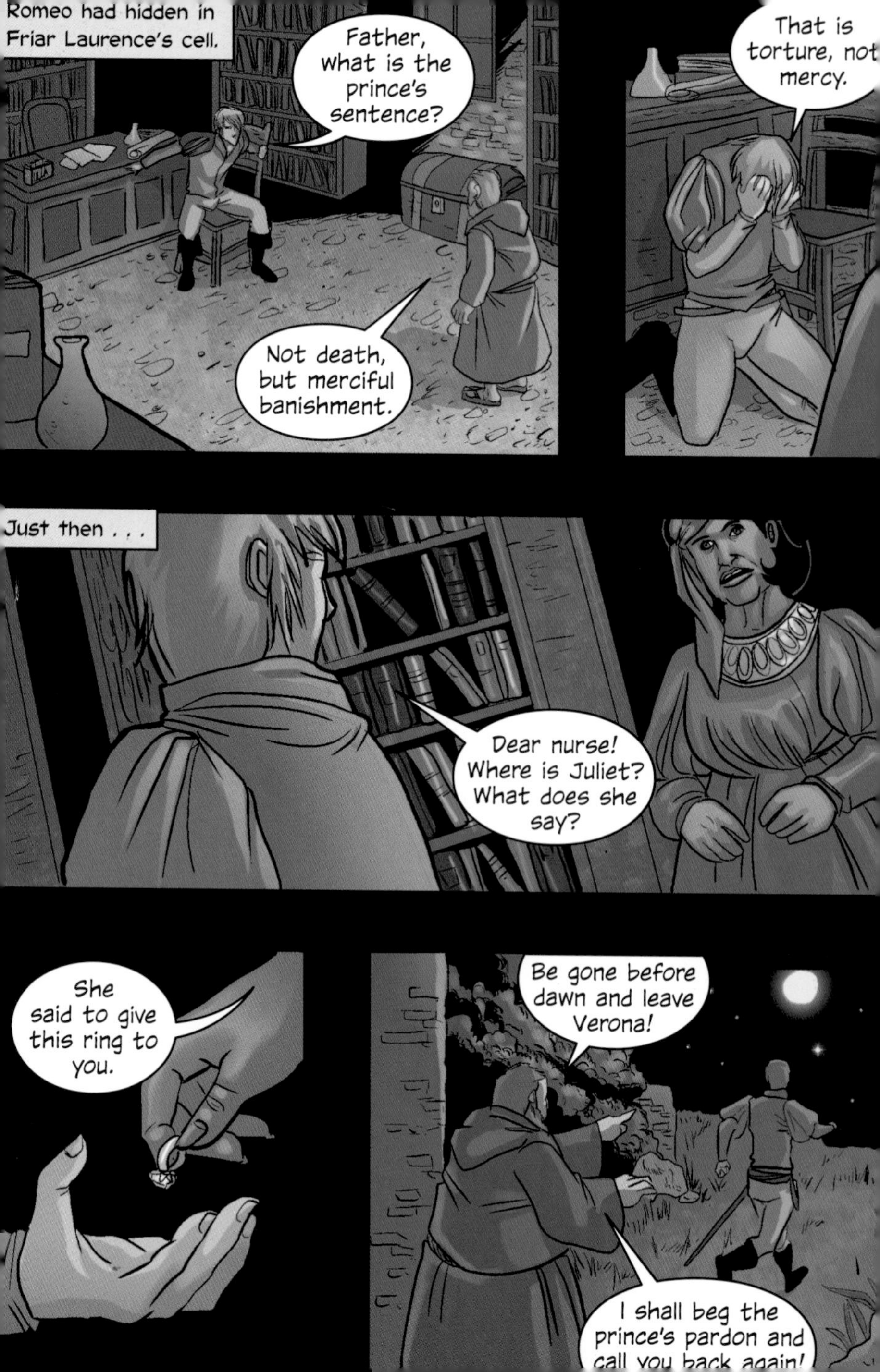

Romeo had hidden in Friar Laurence's cell.
Father, what is the prince's sentence?
Not death, but merciful banishment.
That is torture, not mercy.
Just then . . .
Dear nurse! Where is Juliet? What does she say?
She said to give this ring to you.
Be gone before dawn and leave Verona!
I shall beg the prince's pardon and call you back again!

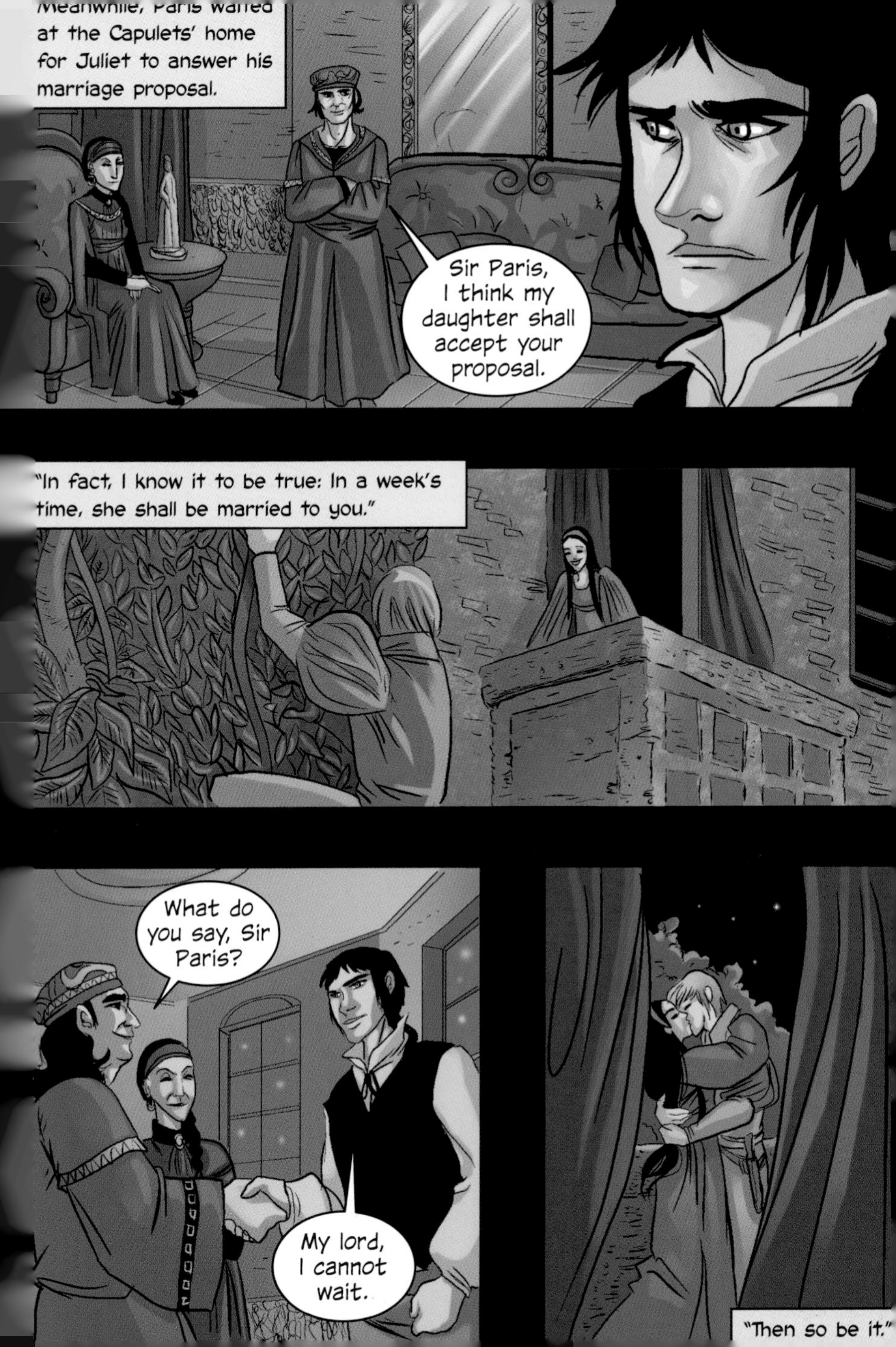
Meanwhile, Paris waited at the Capulets' home for Juliet to answer his marriage proposal.
Sir Paris, I think my daughter shall accept your proposal.
"In fact, I know it to be true: In a week's time, she shall be married to you."
What do you say, Sir Paris?
My lord, I cannot wait.
"Then so be it."

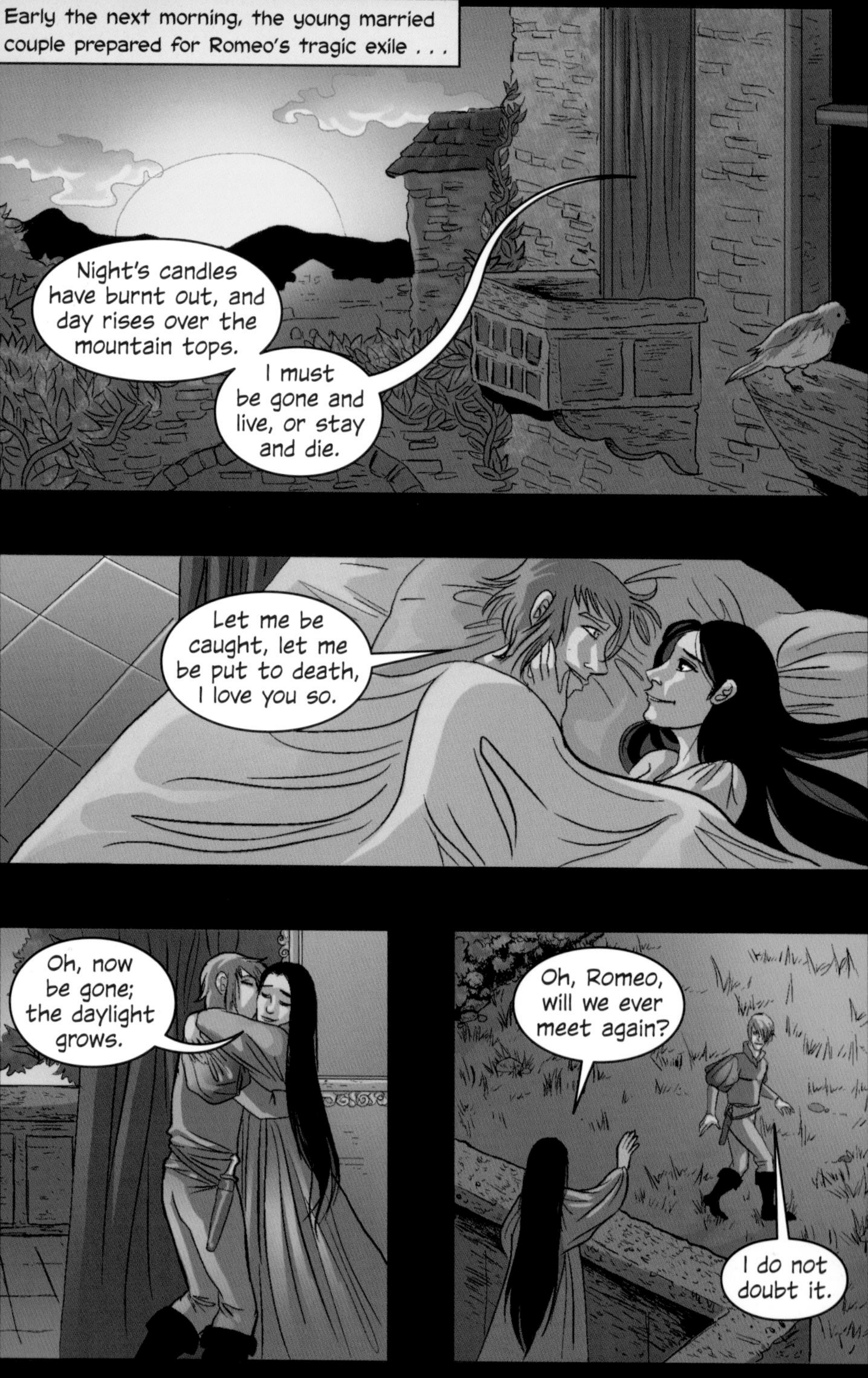
Early the next morning, the young married couple prepared for Romeo's tragic exile . . .
Night's candles have burnt out, and day rises over the mountain tops.
I must be gone and live, or stay and die.
Let me be caught, let me be put to death, I love you so.
Oh, now be gone; the daylight grows.
Oh, Romeo, will we ever meet again?
I do not doubt it.

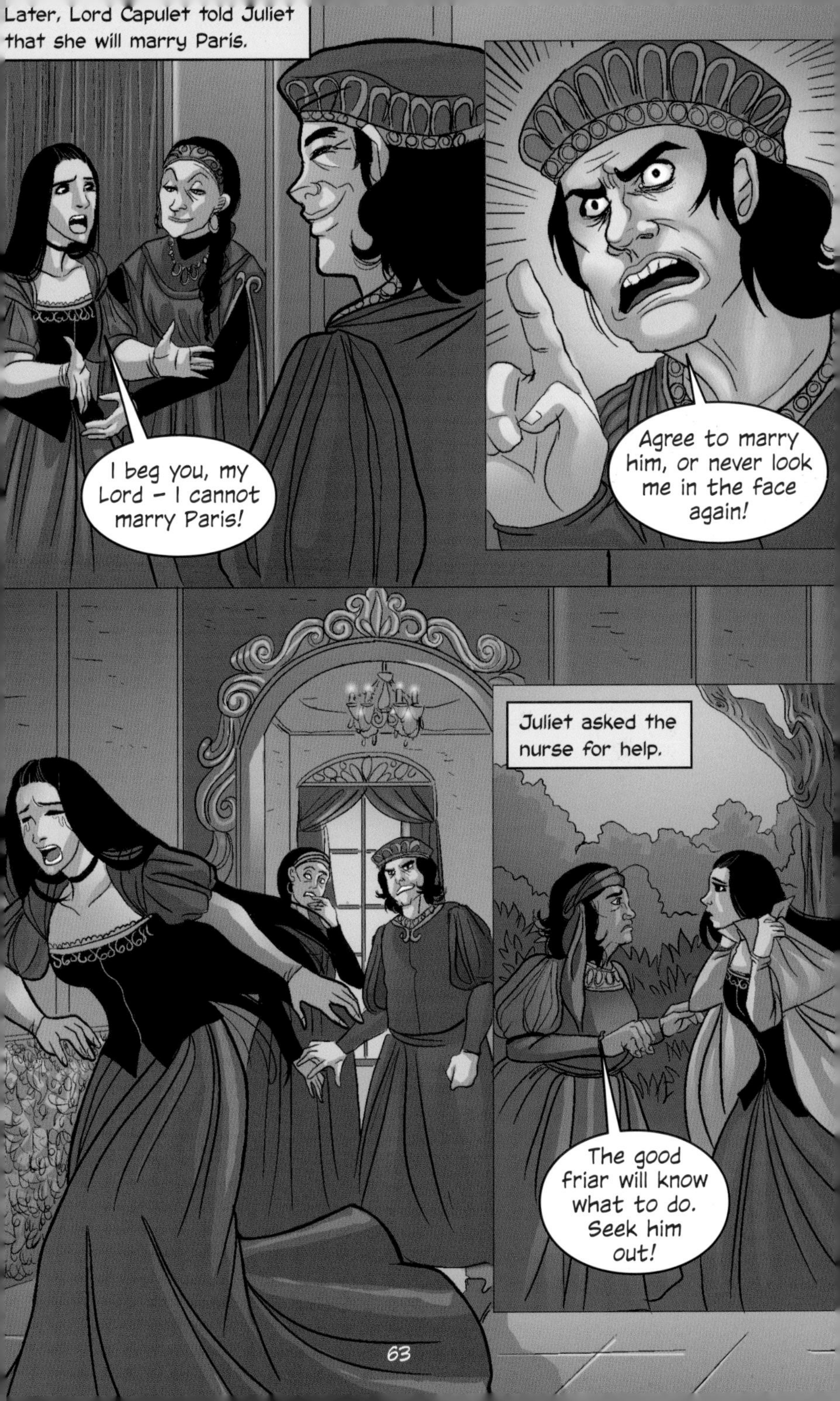
Later, Lord Capulet told Juliet that she will marry Paris.
I beg you, my Lord – I cannot marry Paris!
Agree to marry him, or never look me in the face again!
Juliet asked the nurse for help.
The good friar will know what to do. Seek him out!

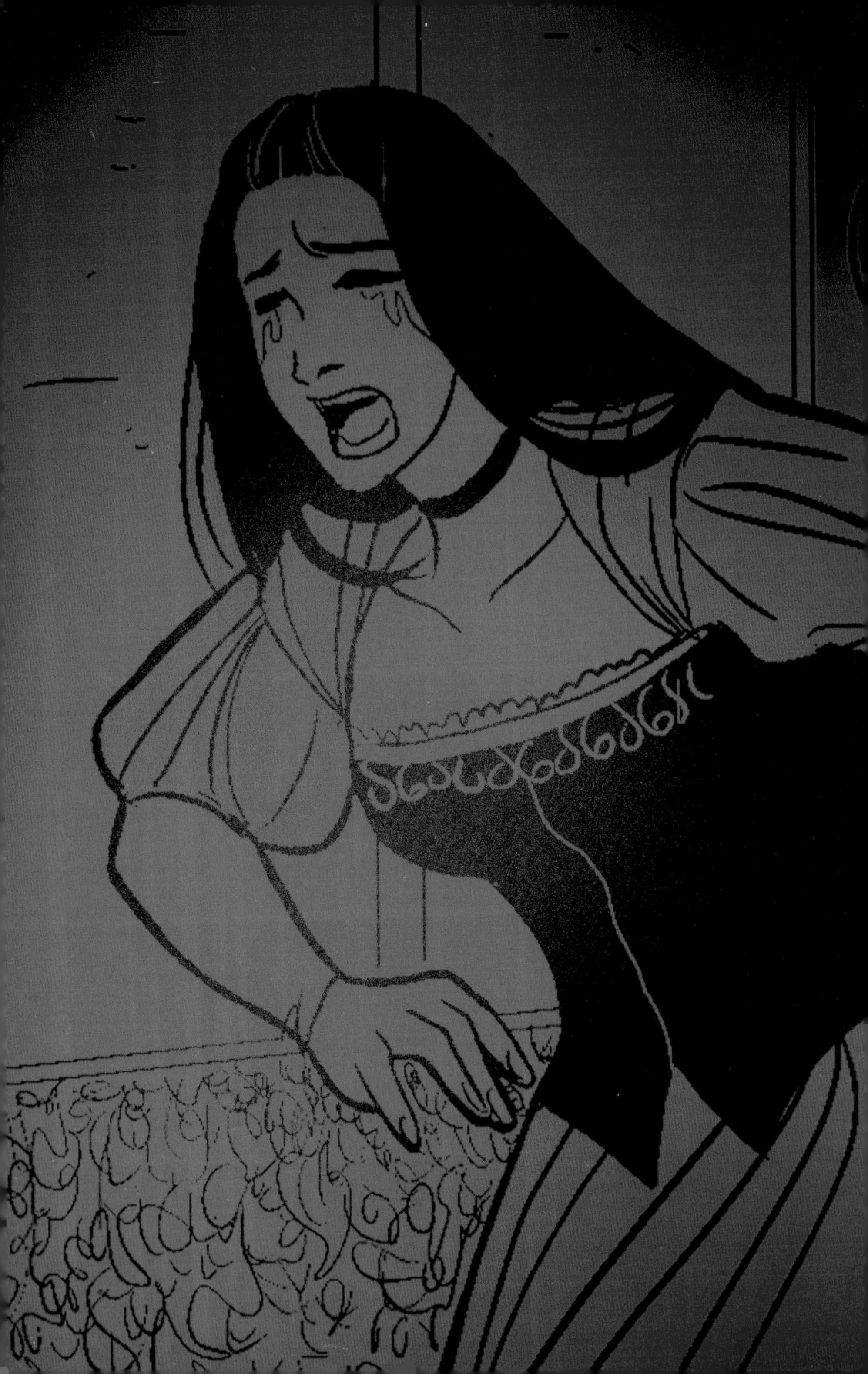

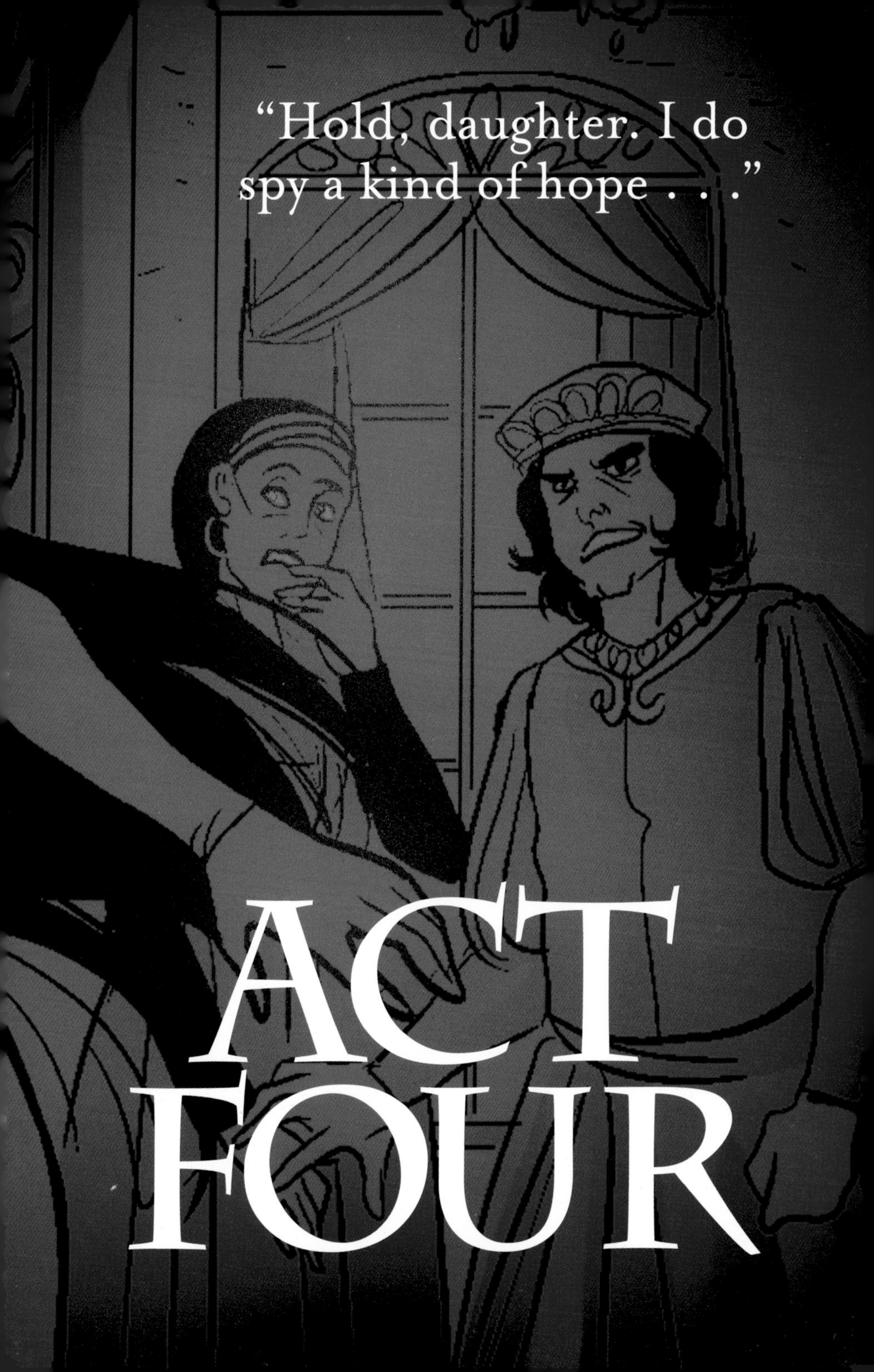

"Hold, daughter. I do spy a kind of hope . . . ."

ACT FOUR

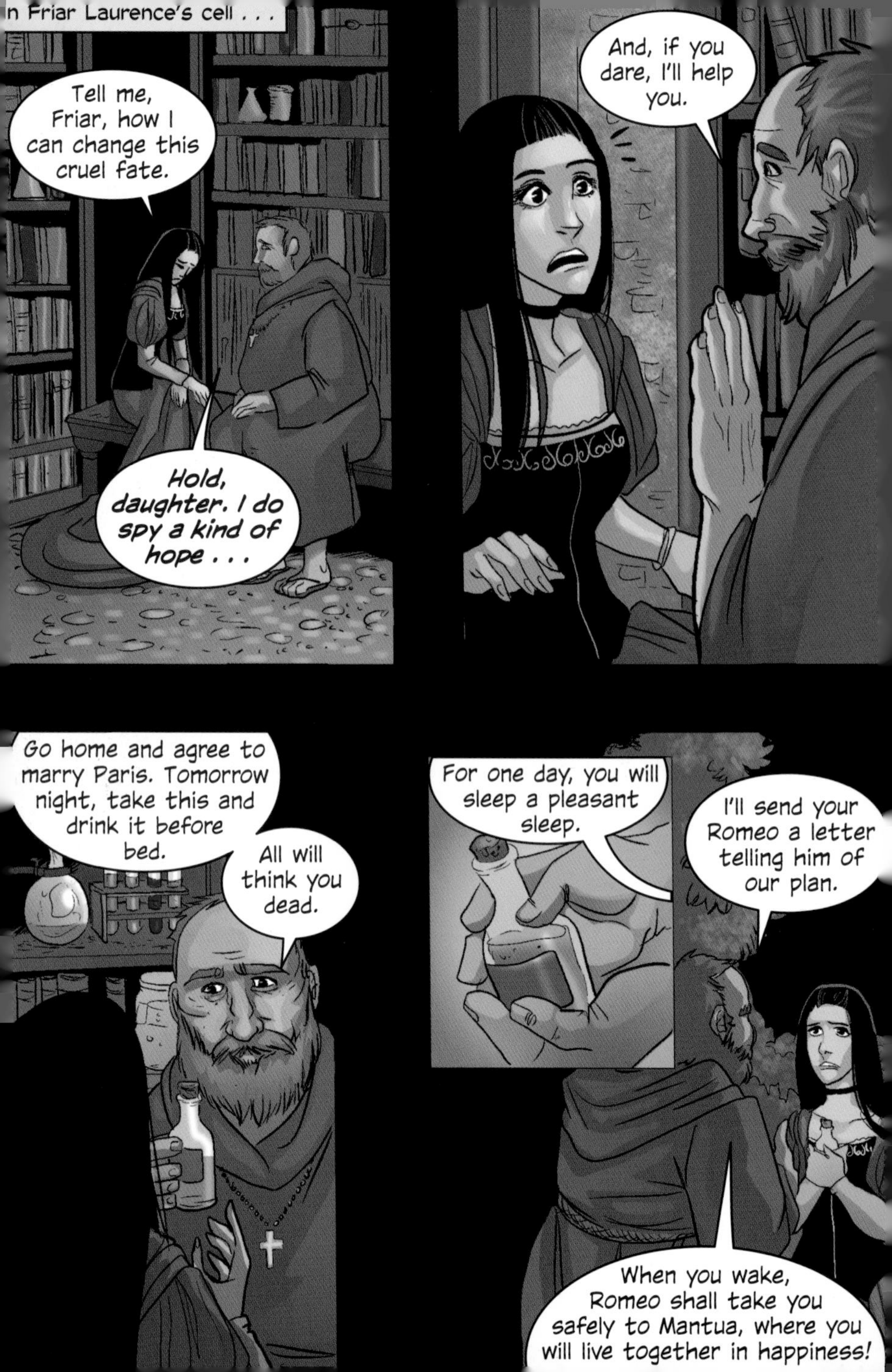

In Friar Laurence's cell . . .
Tell me, Friar, how I can change this cruel fate.
Hold, daughter. I do spy a kind of hope . . .
And, if you dare, I'll help you.
Go home and agree to marry Paris. Tomorrow night, take this and drink it before bed.
All will think you dead.
For one day, you will sleep a pleasant sleep.
I'll send your Romeo a letter telling him of our plan.
When you wake, Romeo shall take you safely to Mantua, where you will live together in happiness!

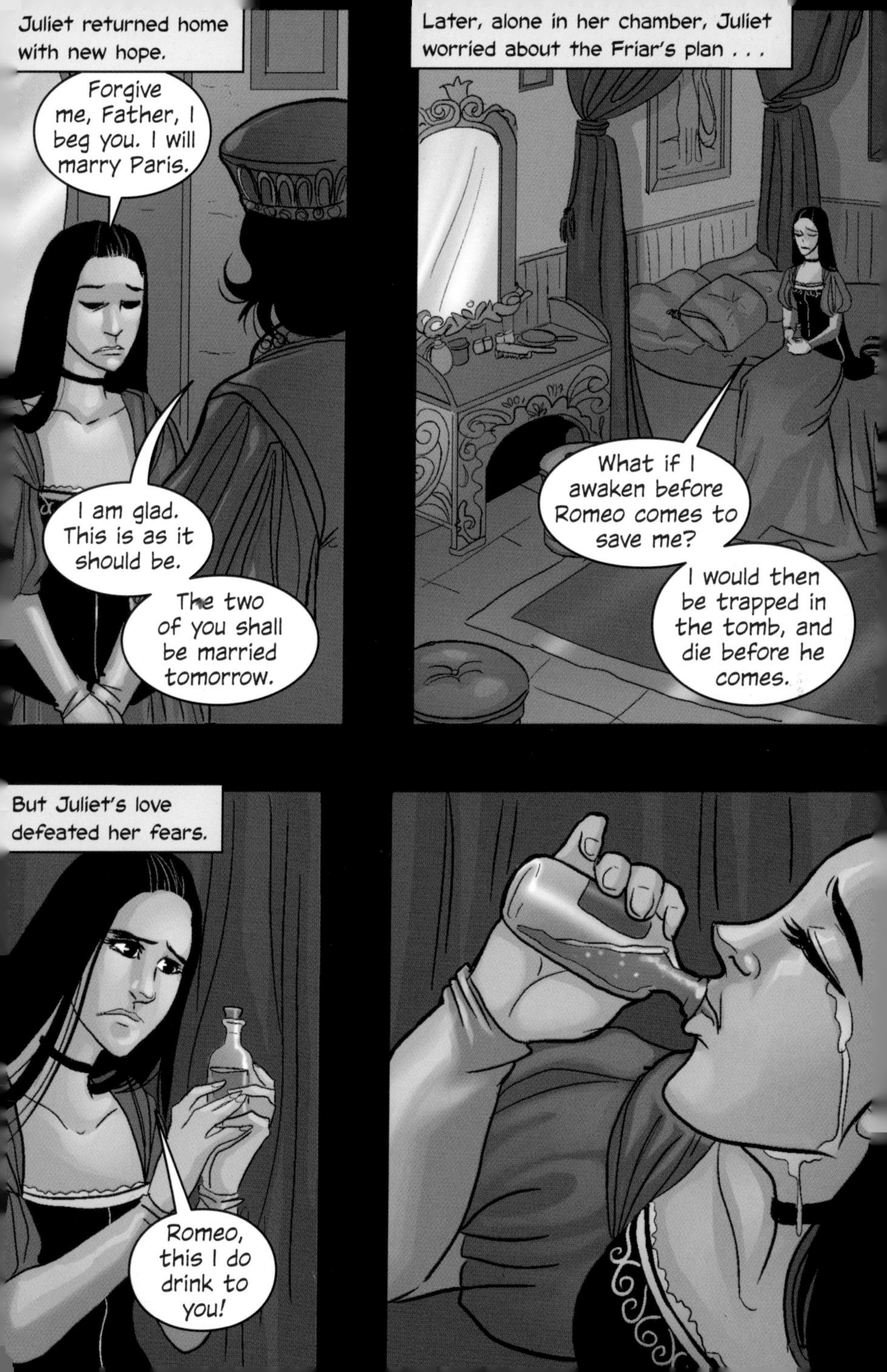
Juliet returned home with new hope.
Forgive me, Father, I beg you. I will marry Paris.
I am glad. This is as it should be.
The two of you shall be married tomorrow.
Later, alone in her chamber, Juliet worried about the Friar's plan . . .
What if I awaken before Romeo comes to save me?
I would then be trapped in the tomb, and die before he comes.
But Juliet's love defeated her fears.
Romeo, this I do drink to you!

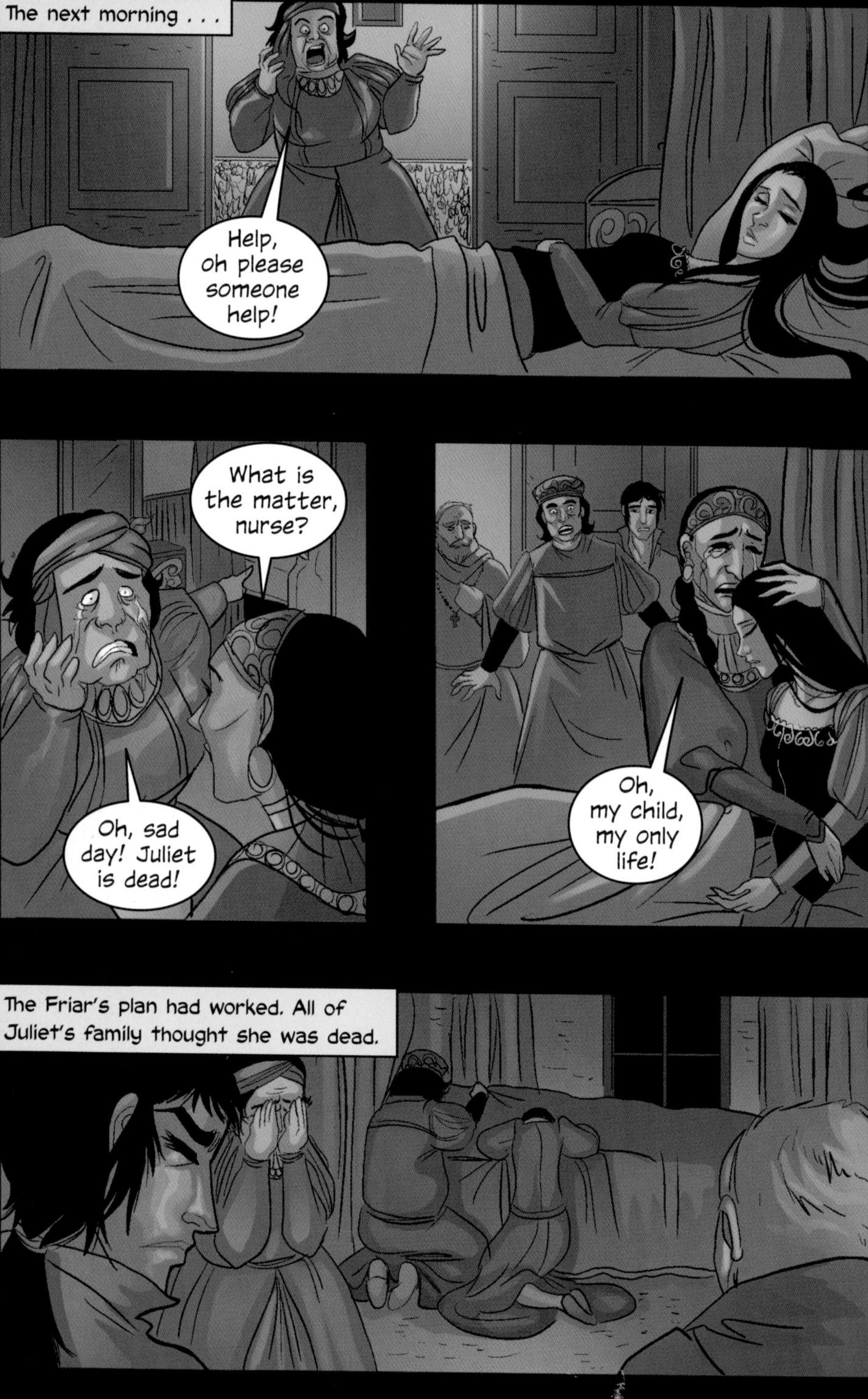
The next morning . . .
Help, oh please someone help!
What is the matter, nurse?
Oh, sad day! Juliet is dead!
Oh, my child, my only life!
The Friar's plan had worked. All of Juliet's family thought she was dead.

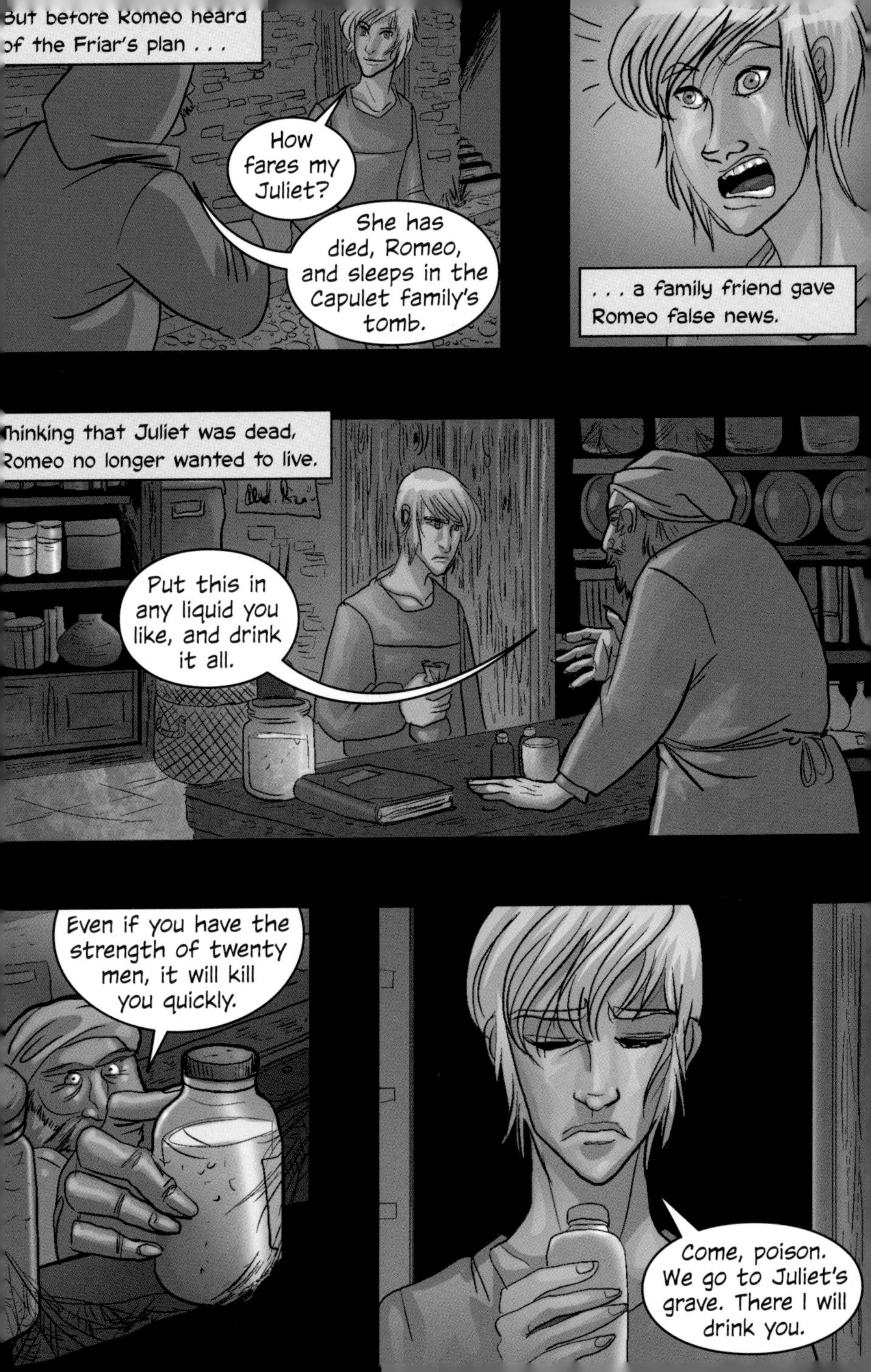
But before Romeo heard of the Friar's plan . . .
How fares my Juliet?
She has died, Romeo, and sleeps in the Capulet family's tomb.
. . . a family friend gave Romeo false news.
Thinking that Juliet was dead, Romeo no longer wanted to live.
Put this in any liquid you like, and drink it all.
Even if you have the strength of twenty men, it will kill you quickly.
Come, poison. We go to Juliet's grave. There I will drink you.

ACT FIVE

"For never was a story of more woe than this of Juliet and her Romeo."

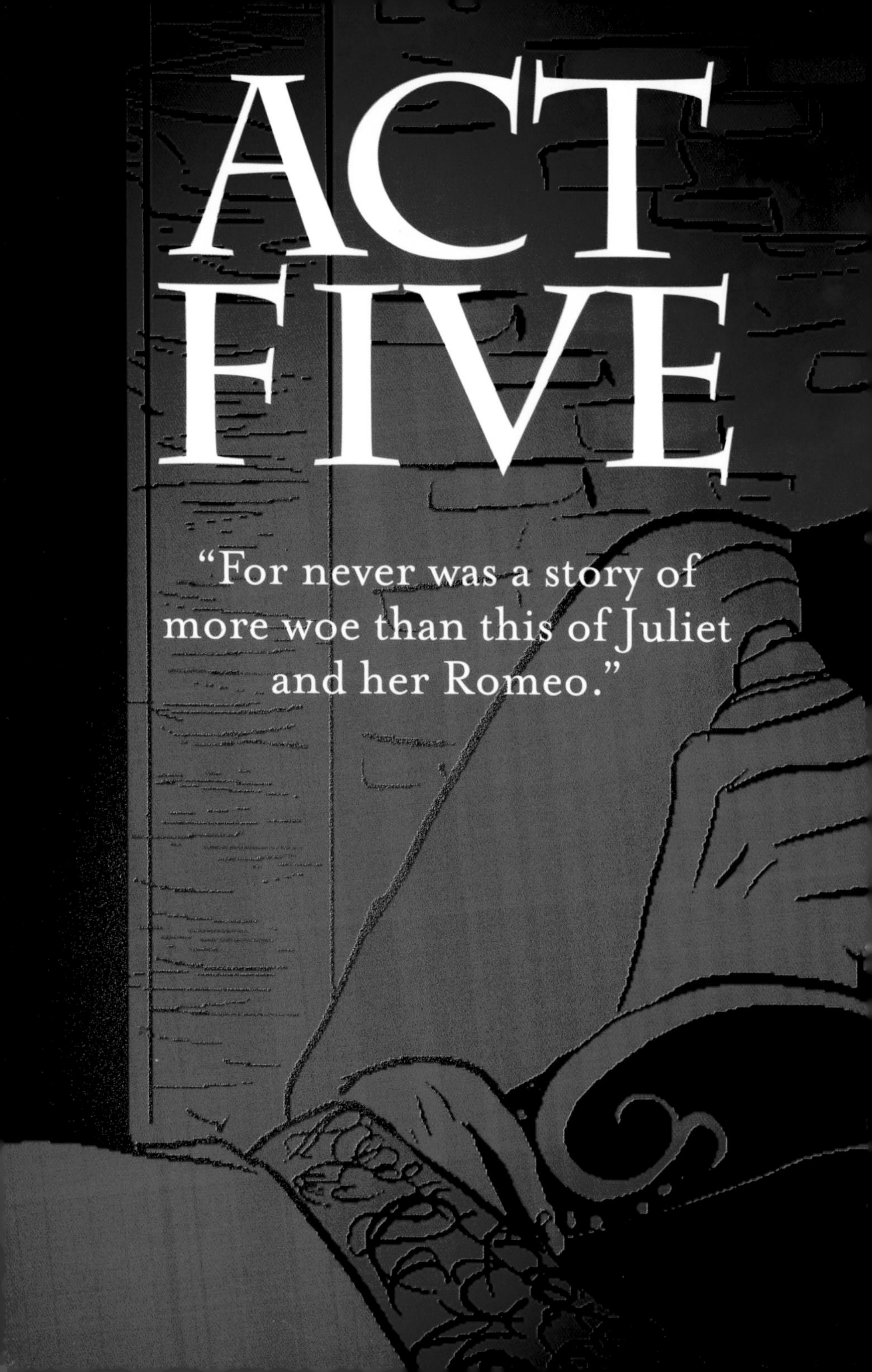

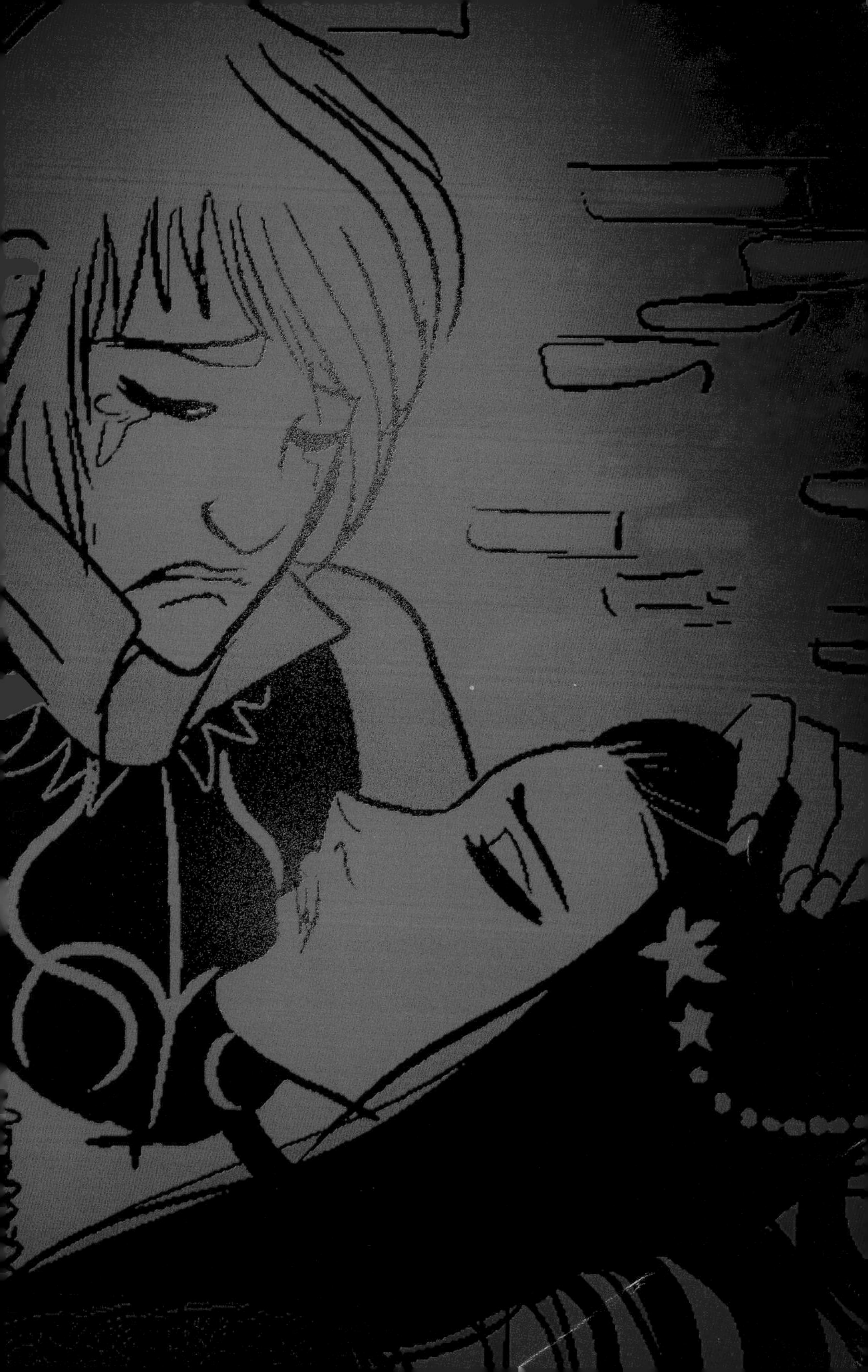

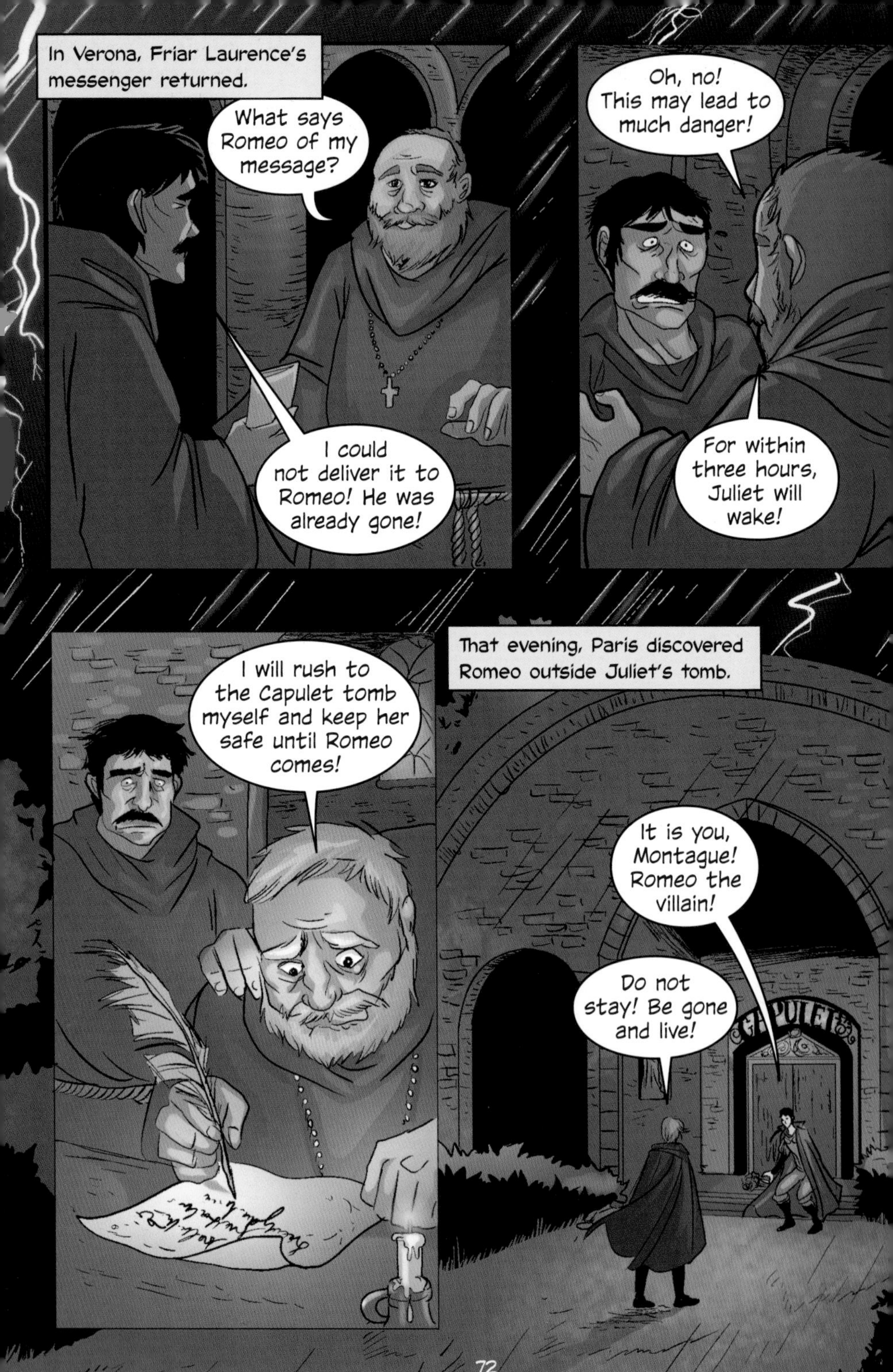
In Verona, Friar Laurence's messenger returned.
What says Romeo of my message?
I could not deliver it to Romeo! He was already gone!
Oh, no! This may lead to much danger!
For within three hours, Juliet will wake!
I will rush to the Capulet tomb myself and keep her safe until Romeo comes!
That evening, Paris discovered Romeo outside Juliet's tomb.
It is you, Montague! Romeo the villain!
Do not stay! Be gone and live!
CAPULET

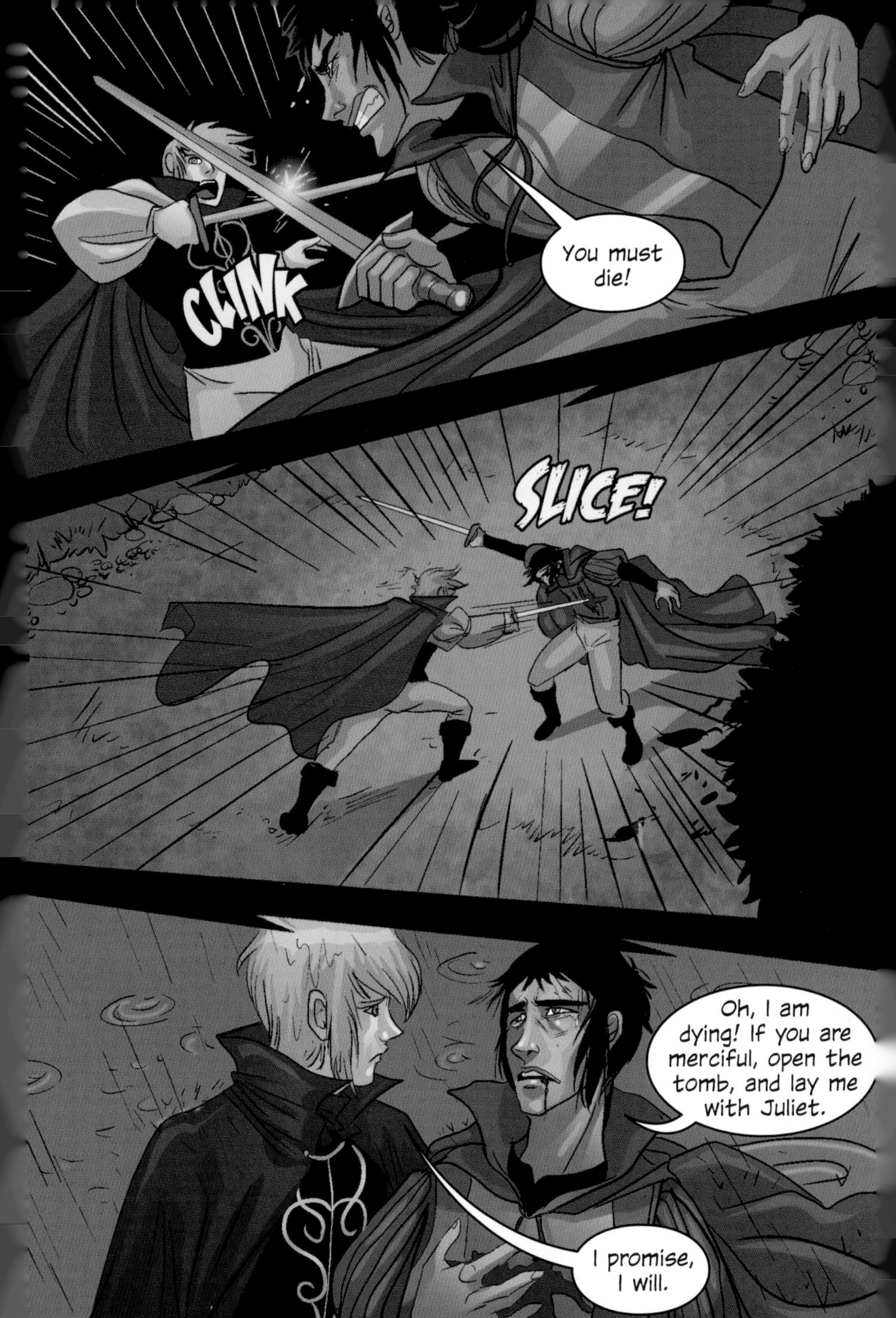
CLINK
You must die!
SLICE!
Oh, I am dying! If you are merciful, open the tomb, and lay me with Juliet.
I promise, I will.

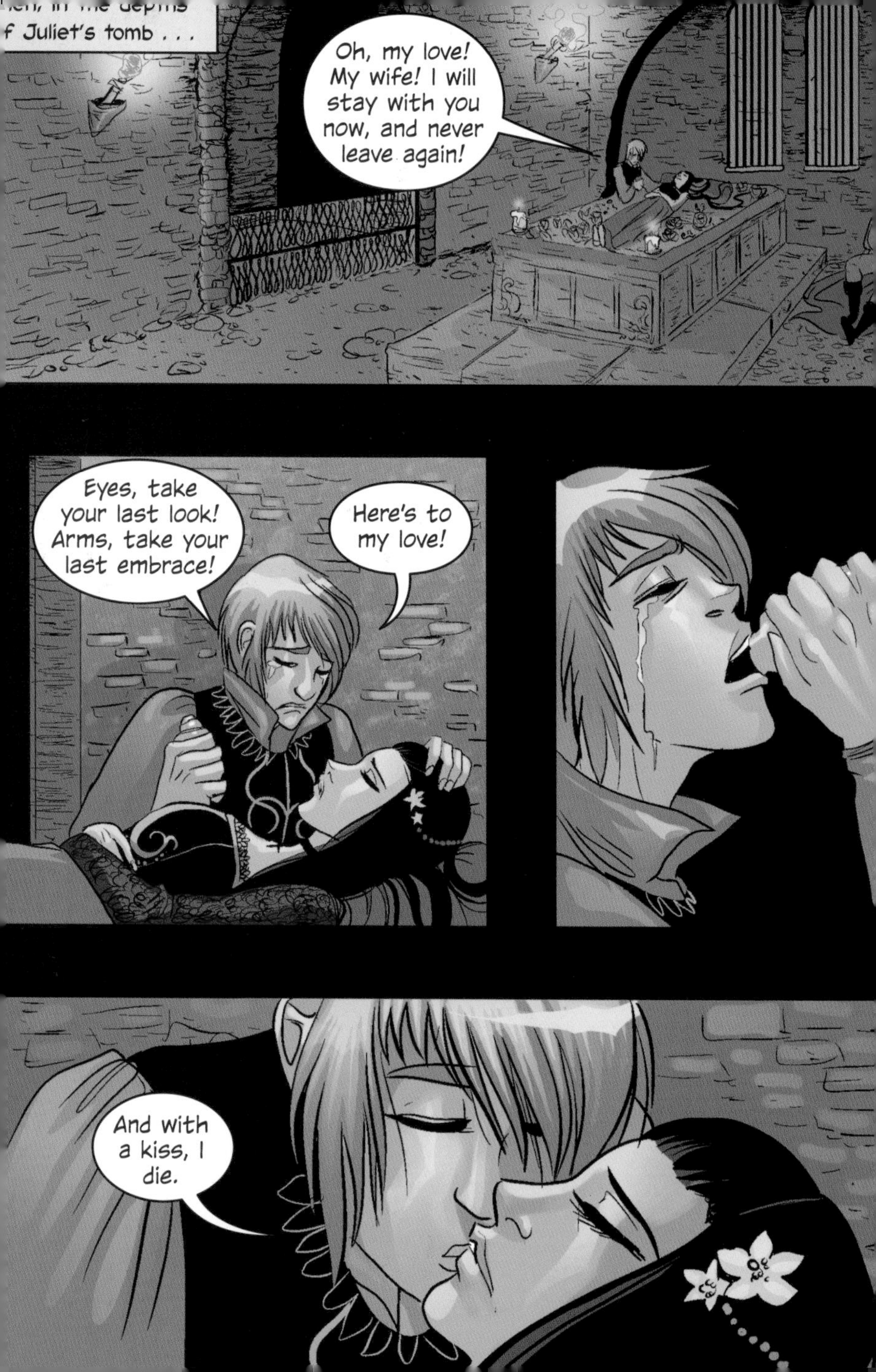
Juliet's tomb . . .
Oh, my love! My wife! I will stay with you now, and never leave again!
Eyes, take your last look! Arms, take your last embrace!
Here's to my love!
And with a kiss, I die.

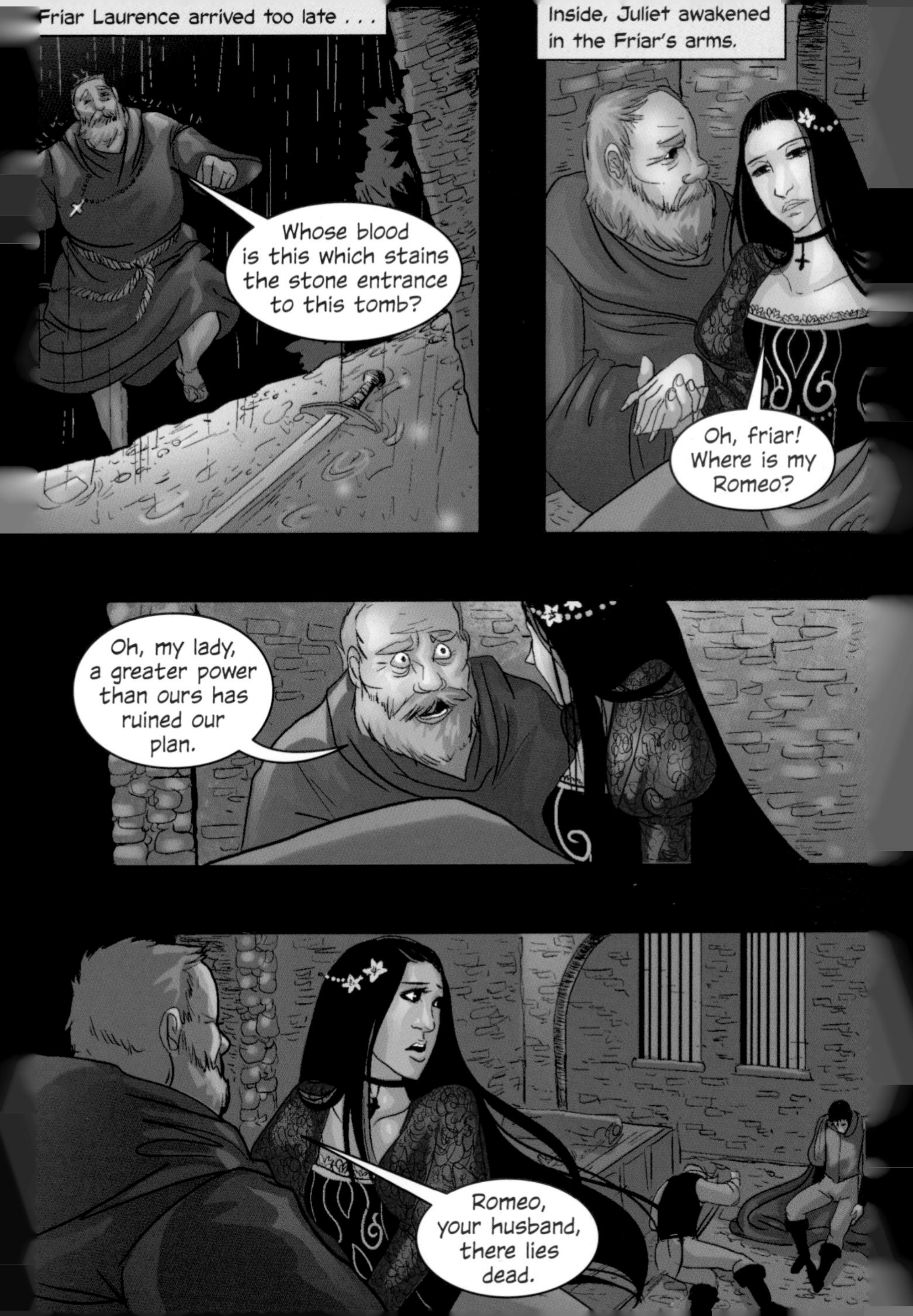
Friar Laurence arrived too late . . .
Whose blood is this which stains the stone entrance to this tomb?
Inside, Juliet awakened in the Friar's arms.
Oh, friar! Where is my Romeo?
Oh, my lady, a greater power than ours has ruined our plan.
Romeo, your husband, there lies dead.

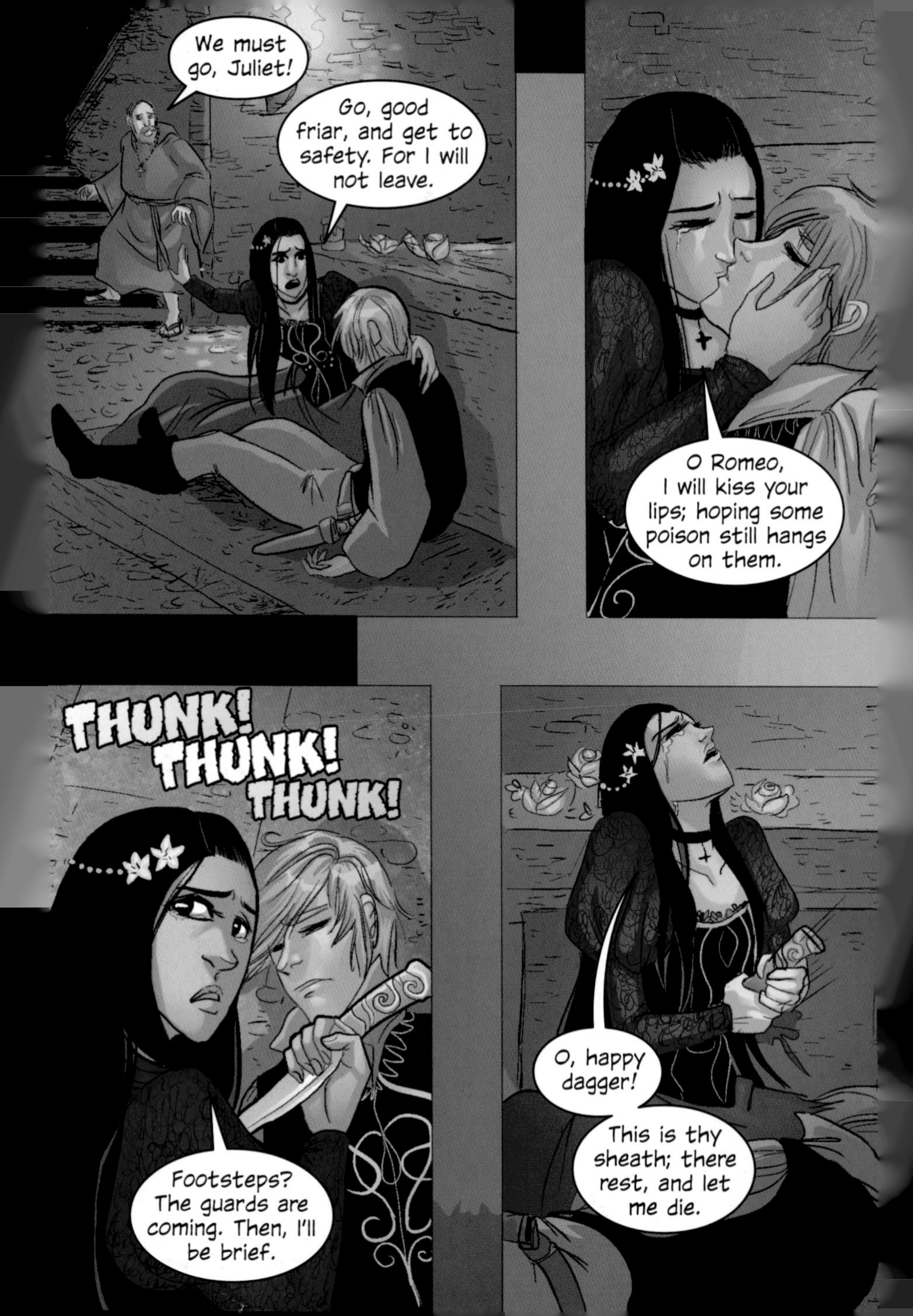
We must go, Juliet!
Go, good friar, and get to safety. For I will not leave.
O Romeo, I will kiss your lips; hoping some poison still hangs on them.
THUNK! THUNK! THUNK!
Footsteps? The guards are coming. Then, I'll be brief.
O, happy dagger!
This is thy sheath; there rest, and let me die.

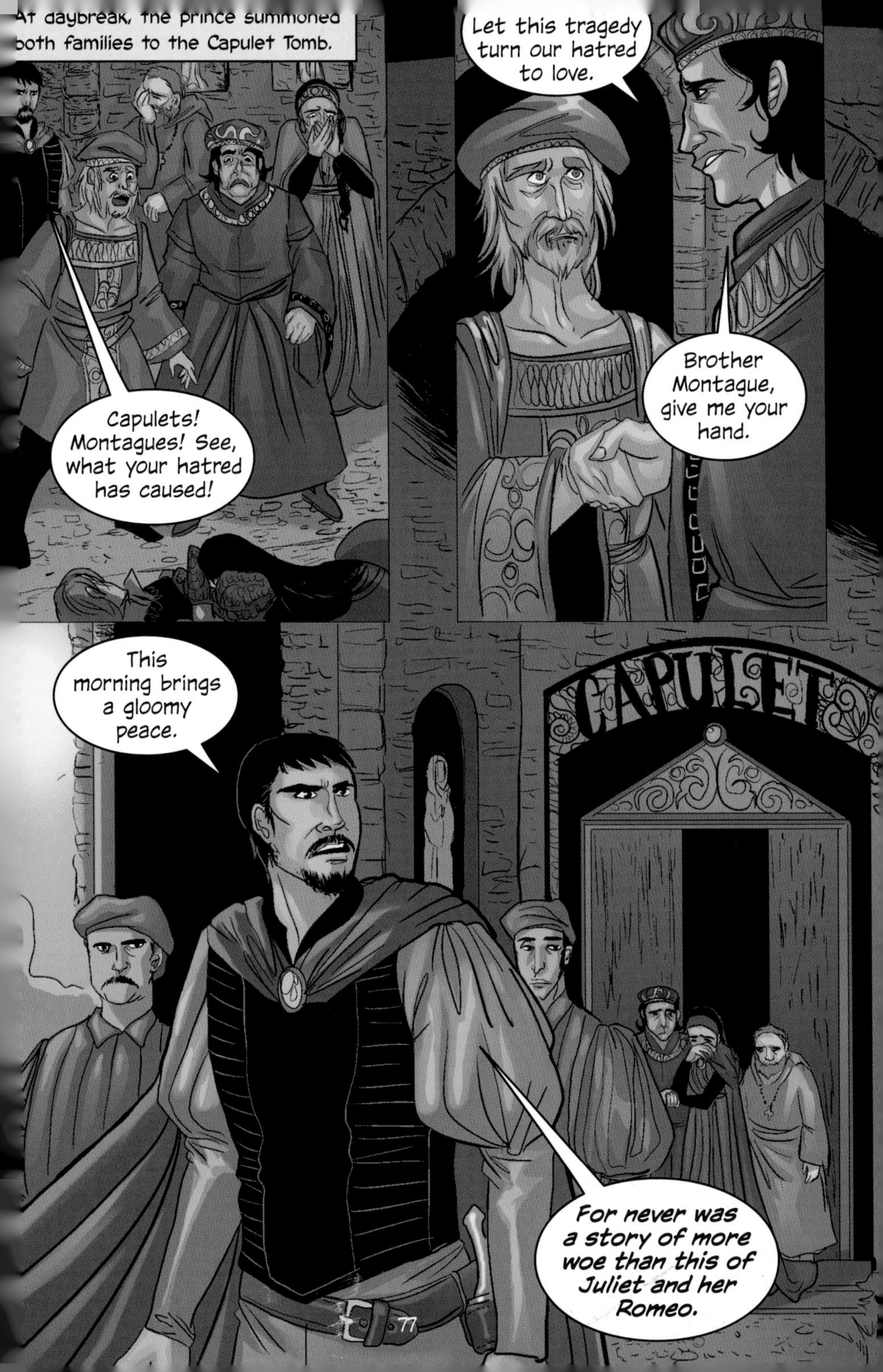
At daybreak, the prince summoned both families to the Capulet Tomb.
Capulets! Montagues! See, what your hatred has caused!
Let this tragedy turn our hatred to love.
Brother Montague, give me your hand.
CAPULET
This morning brings a gloomy peace.
For never was a story of more woe than this of Juliet and her Romeo.

ABOUT THE RETELLING AUTHOR

Since 1986, **Martin Powell** has been a freelance writer. He has written hundreds of stories, many of which have been published by Disney, Marvel, Tekno Comix, Moonstone Books, and others. In 1989, Powell received an Eisner Award nomination for his graphic novel *Scarlet in Gaslight*. This award is one of the highest comic book honors.

ABOUT THE ILLUSTRATORS

Eva Cabrera is a sequential artist born in Jalapa, Veracruz, Mexico. She is currently the Art Director of Neggi Studio (videogames) and an illustrator at Zombie Studio. She also illustrates comic books for Protobunker Studio as the main artist for *El Arsenal: Been Caught Stealing*. She has won several comic-related national contests and has participated in various art expos. In her spare time, Eva feeds her addiction to coffee and the Internet.

Jorge Gonzalez was born in Monterrey, Mexico, in 1982. Since then, he has dedicated several years of his life to the comic book industry. Jorge began his career as a colorist for the graphic novel retellings of *The Time Machine* and *Journey to the Center of the Earth*. In 2006, Jorge, along with several other artists, established Protobunker Studio, where he currently works as a colorist.

ABOUT WILLIAM SHAKESPEARE

William Shakespeare's true date of birth is unknown, but it is celebrated on April 23rd, 1564. He was born in Stratford-upon-Avon, England. He was the third of eight children to his parents, John and Mary.

At age 18, William married a woman named Anne Hathaway on November 27th, 1582. He and Anne had three children together, including twins. After that point, Shakespeare's history is somewhat of a mystery. Not much is known about that period of his life, until 1592 when his plays first graced theater stages in London, England.

From 1594 onward, Shakespeare performed his plays with a stage company called the Lord Chamberlain's Men (later known as the King's Men). They soon became the top playing company in all of London, earning the favor of Queen Elizabeth and King James I along the way.

Shakespeare retired in 1613, and died at age 52 on April 23rd, 1616. He was buried at Holy Trinity Church in Stratford. The epitaph on his grave curses any person who disturbs it. Translated to modern English, part of it reads:

> *Blessed be the man that spares these stones,*
> *And cursed be he who moves my bones.*

Over a period of 25 years, Shakespeare wrote more than 40 works, including poems, plays, and prose. His plays have been performed all over the world and in every major language.

THE HISTORY BEHIND THE PLAY

Romeo and Juliet is one of Shakespeare's most popular plays. It was written sometime between the years 1591 and 1595.

Shakespeare's *Romeo and Juliet* was inspired by several old, tragic love stories. One of these is an Italian tale written in 1562, called *The Tragical History of Romeus and Juliet*. Another is called "Pyramus and Thisbe," from Ovid's *Metamorphoses*, which is also performed as a play-within-a-play in Shakespeare's *A Midsummer Night's Dream*.

This play contains several soliloquies, or speeches where a character speaks out loud to himself or herself. When Juliet starts to speak her soliloquy on page 36, she does not know Romeo is listening. He, too, gives a soliloquy, starting on page 34, before talking to Juliet.

Most of the early performances of Shakespeare's plays featured only male actors. The roles of female characters, like Juliet, were played by men who wore wigs and dresses.

Romeo and Juliet is one of the most popular plays of all time. Even today, it is performed in theaters all over the world. *Romeo and Juliet* has also been made into several movies, musicals, ballets, operas — and graphic novels like this one.

SHAKESPEAREAN LANGUAGE

Shakespeare's writing is powerful and memorable — and sometimes difficult to understand. Many lines in his plays can be read in different ways or can have multiple meanings. Also, the English language was not standardized in Shakespeare's time, so the way he spelled words was not always the same as we spell them nowadays. However, Shakespeare still influences the way we write and speak today. Below are some of his more famous phrases that have become part of our language.

FAMOUS LINES FROM ROMEO & JULIET

"A pair of star-cross'd lovers . . ." (Prologue)

SPEAKER: Chorus

MODERN INTERPRETATION: **A pair of young people fall in love and suffer because fate is against them.**

EXPLANATION: Long ago, people believed that our fates were written in the stars. In this line, the chorus (or narrator) explains that the stars have turned against Romeo and Juliet's love, dooming their relationship from the start.

"O Romeo, Romeo! Wherefore art thou Romeo?"
(Act II, Scene II)

SPEAKER: Juliet

MODERN INTERPRETATION: **Oh, Romeo, why do you have to be Romeo Montague?**

EXPLANATION: Juliet, a Capulet, wishes that Romeo was not a Montague. She is unaware that he is nearby, listening to her soliloquy. Also, "wherefore" does not mean "where" as many people mistakenly believe — it actually means "why."

"A plague o' both the houses!" (Act III, Scene I)

SPEAKER: Mercutio

MODERN INTERPRETATION: **May a plague, or sickness, curse both of your families.**

EXPLANATION: Mercutio, after being stabbed by Tybalt Capulet because Romeo Montague interfered, blames both their feuding families for his death.

"Hold, daughter. I do spy a kind of hope . . ." (Act IV, Scene I)

SPEAKER: Friar Laurence

MODERN INTERPRETATION: **Wait a second, young lady, I see some hope.**

EXPLANATION: Friar Laurence attempts to calm Juliet by telling her that there is still hope for her and Romeo's love. He then warns her that it will be dangerous, and they must act quickly.

"For never was a story of more woe than this of Juliet and her Romeo." (Act V, Scene III)

SPEAKER: The prince

MODERN INTERPRETATION: **There was never a story with more pain and suffering than the story of Romeo and Juliet's relationship.**

EXPLANATION: The prince explains that the tragic tale of Romeo and Juliet's love, and their sad deaths, is made even more tragic by the unlucky circumstances surrounding them.

DISCUSSION QUESTIONS

1. Romeo and Juliet fall in love at first sight. Do you believe in love at first sight? Why or why not?

2. This graphic novel has many illustrations. Which page is your favorite? Why?

3. Juliet's parents don't approve of her love of Romeo. Does your family disapprove of anything you do?

1. The Capulets and the Montagues hate each other. Can you think of some ways for the two families to learn to get along? What would you do if you were Romeo or Juliet? Write about how you'd put an end to the family feud.

2. Romeo and Juliet meet at a costume ball, or party. Imagine that you're going to attend a costume party. What kind of outfit would you wear? Write about it, then draw a picture of yourself in your outfit.

3. Which character is most to blame for the deaths of Romeo and Juliet? Was it Friar Laurence? Tybalt? Romeo? Juliet? Someone else? Explain your answer.

INTRODUCING ANOTHER SHAKESPEARE GRAPHIC NOVEL . . .

JULIUS CAESAR

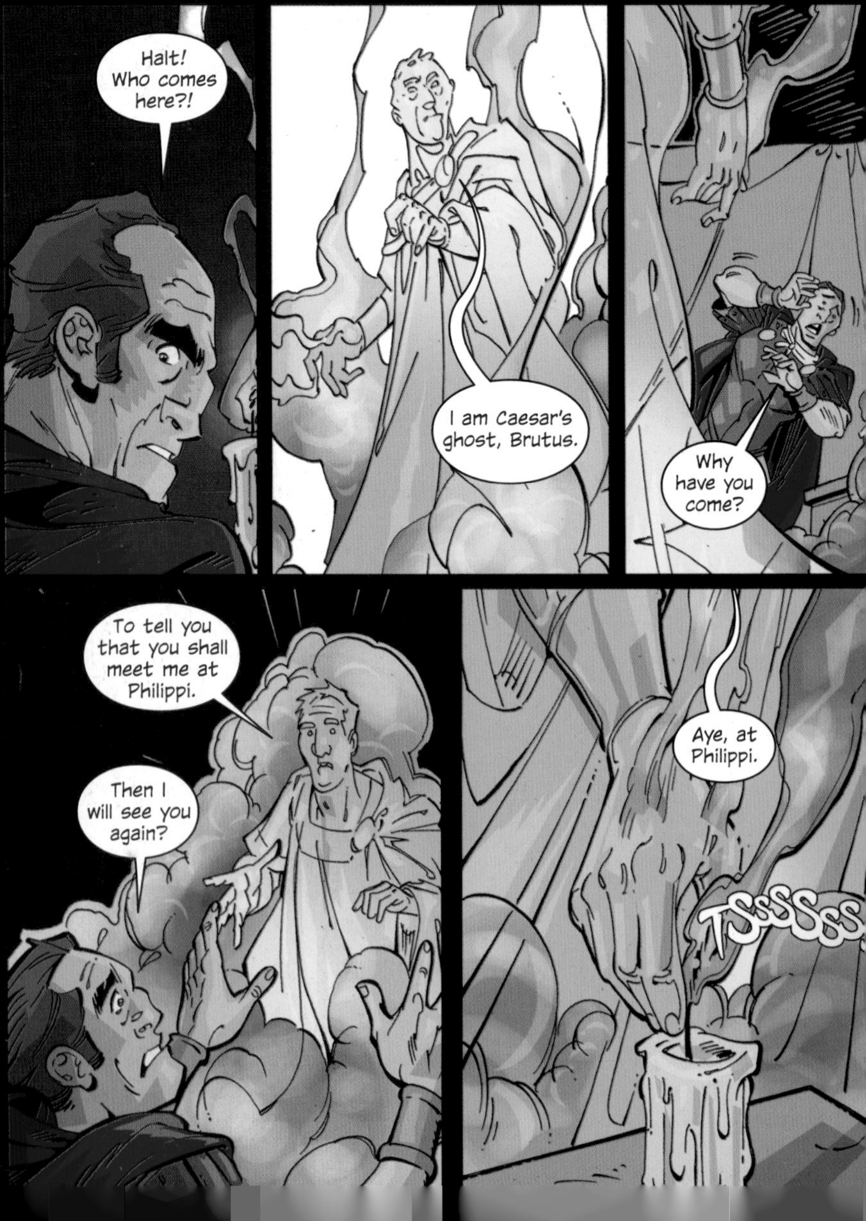
Halt! Who comes here?!
I am Caesar's ghost, Brutus.
Why have you come?
To tell you that you shall meet me at Philippi.
Then I will see you again?
Aye, at Philippi.
TSSSSSS